THE RIVAL'S PACT

ALBERT HOM

CONTENTS

PROLOGUE

Death is in this room with me. I can feel him standing at my shoulder. Watching me. This first kill, I think to myself, is going to be the beginning of my long friendship with him.

Death tells me I should run. I know I should run. I know I should get as far away from the body as I can. But I'm frozen, with my eyes locked on the councilman's lifeless form.

Conrad didn't give me any details about this kill. He just told me to get in and get out of Councilman Vick's house as quickly as possible. Not that Conrad is worried about me getting caught. We both know Conrad doesn't bother with people if he thinks they won't succeed.

With quiet movements, I bring my switchblade back out, cutting the brand all of Conrad's assassins use to mark a kill into the body.

This is my first time seeing the brand on an actual body, and I'm surprised by how revolted I find the mark to be as the blood pools out of the wound.

Once the proper cuts are made, I leave the body on the floor of the bathroom.

It would be easy for me to exit through the same window that I came in through, but something stops me.

I pad across the tiled floor into the councilman's bedchamber.

Soft breathing indicates the body of his wife asleep in their bed.

I feel an odd sort of longing to wake her and apologize for the havoc I've just caused on her and her family's lives. But I know better than to wake her. Conrad could easily kill me for doing such a thing. It would show the weakness he hates to see so much in his assassins.

With a small sigh of regret, I walk out of the councilman's room. Instead, making my way through his home, looking at paintings of the councilman and his family. I wonder what this man has done to earn one of Conrad's death warrants?

A sound comes from upstairs. I whip around, taking in the staircase behind me. Nobody's there.

Before I do anything I might regret, I exit through the front door. Leaving it unlocked behind me.

After leaving the councilman's house, I walk through Mardon's streets in the early morning mist.

It's still too early for the street lamps to have been lit, but Mardon is never truly dark anyway. I find myself tracing my way up familiar streets till I reach the gates to the palace, where the King and his family have lived for years.

Conrad loves to send all of his assassins out here to look at the King's palace and talk to us about how Mordon used to be a republic. But how ever since King Seer's rain began twenty years ago, our country has been falling apart. Conrad thinks he can change all of this once we kill our way to the top and he becomes the new king.

Just before sunup, I find myself wandering back home to The Swarm, where all of us assassins live.

As I walk, my thoughts keep wandering back to the way I killed the councilman. I feel horrible about my first assassination, though these feelings come as no surprise. Conrad has told all of his assassins many times that we might have conflicting emotions about our first kill, but with time those feelings will fade and we will be able to see the beauty of taking unworthy lives out of this world.

I guess that feeling just hasn't come to me yet.

As I approach The Swarm, I find myself liking the feeling of being outside of my home without the constant threat of Conrad getting mad at me for being out too late.

Conrad always keeps a close eye on all of us assassins. I suppose if I were in charge of the fifty most deadly killers in the kingdom, I too would keep a close eye on them.

Actually, Conrad is in charge of many groups of assassins, not just the fifty of us here at the Swarm in Mardon's capital. He has smaller groups of killers all around the kingdom, although I've never met anyone from any of Corand's other gangs.

With each step I take, my mind can't move on from the fact that I just killed someone. I feel that at any moment someone is going to leap out and arrest me for the murder that's bound to make the paper tomorrow morning.

After what feels like ages, I finally reach the front gate leading up to The Swarm. It's a large house with gold edging and a well manicured front lawn that none of the Swarm members are ever allowed to step on unless leaving or returning from a mission.

Passing the front door we're not allowed to use, I go right around to the back, opening the soundproof cellar door that leads right into the large and very loud basement of the house.

I've lived in this basement ever since last year, when Conrad found me on the streets attempting to be a thief. He'd immediately taken me here to come live at The Swarm with a new sort of family.

I hadn't known what I was getting into then. I'd just wanted to belong to something. To be part of a family.

Now I sure belonged to something. It's just a very blood-thirsty something.

Noise is everywhere the moment I enter the basement.

For a brief moment nobody notices me.

"Look who's back! Little Miss Perfect!" Shouts a booming female voice after a moment. Quincy's dark, heavy arm drapes over my shoulder as she gives me an overly affectionate pat on the back.

If I hadn't just returned from killing someone, I would have laughed and smiled at her. But I can't bring myself to. I feel... stained in an odd way by the blood I've just shed.

"So how'd it go?" Kent, another member of The Swarm, asks from where he's playing poker with Qace.

I shrug, "I did it."

They all go quiet for a moment before Qace, not looking up from his game with Kent, says, "It'll get easier to kill. But at least now you won't have to worry about Conrad killing you for knowing too much. You've officially joined The Swarm, Isha."

"Yeah," another voice strikes in, "but now she'll just get killed by one hundred other factors. Like getting caught and arrested. But hey, at least Conrad won't kill her." It's Jax. "But who knows, she might just be daydreaming and fall off a building all by herself." He winks at me.

I give Jax my most putrid glare.

"Shut up." I snap at him.

Jax joined Conrad the same time I did, though he's two years my elder and won't let me forget it. His soul factor of enjoyment in life is being a pain in my side.

Quincy shoots Jax a glare before turning to me, "Don't listen to that cocky frog, you're a member now! That's all that matters. Now Conrad wants ya to go see him, then get to bed and don't let all of the others pester ya with questions; ya hear me?"

I nod as I walk away to meet with the man who saved me from the slums of the city but has now indentured me to a life I didn't exactly choose.

Conrad is the only one of us who lives upstairs. I walk through the well polished upstairs rooms with tapestries, art, flowers, crisp furniture, and sculptures till I reach the door to his office.

Taking a deep breath, I ready myself to knock. But before I can, a clean assertive voice cuts through the air, "Come in."

I learned long ago not to question Conrad about how he always seems a step ahead of the rest of the world.

I walk into his office.

Conrad sits at his desk, the tall windows behind him blaring the morning sun into my eyes.

I wait for him to address me first, not looking at him until he speaks my name.

For a long moment, Conrad reads through the paper in front of him. Finally with barely a glance up he says, "Isha? Report please."

It's not a question.

I picture the councilman's dead body frozen and lifeless on the ground. I feel sick at the thought, but I shove it down, telling myself that I don't regret what I did.

I am officially a member of the Swarm now.

That's all that matters.

"I killed counselor Vick." I state calmly.

Conrad's eyes feel like knives over my skin. "And?"

I gulp, "And what?"

"And what did you think? Would you like to join my cause to bring down the King?"

Years ahead of me of killing and killing and... killing.

No. No, I do not want to join The Swarm. I want to go back home.

But my home is gone.

The Swarm is all I have left.

Qace was wrong. If I say no in this moment Conrad will be the one to kill me.

I nod with as much assurance as I can, "Yes."

A long moment of silence follows that simple word before Conrad finally speaks, "You're a smart girl, Isha. That's why I picked it up off the streets. You should be more grateful."

He says picked like he hadn't stumbled across me trying to pick his pocket, desperate for food.

I simply nod.

"It will get easier," he muses, seeing in my eyes how hard it was for me to kill someone today. "You'll learn the beauty of taking unworthy lives out of this world."

I give one more nod before I'm released from his presence, awaiting the new life ahead of me filled with violence and death.

But at least I'll live.

Besides, Death, with all of his faults, is at the very least a loyal friend.

CHAPTER 1

The air smells foul here, but it's not shocking to me given that I grew up on this side of town.

Jax, on the other hand, has never had the pleasure of being raised in this dump.

"Aces, I wish I didn't have a nose to smell this." He mutters under his breath.

I smirk up at him, "I'd be happy to cut it off for you if you like."

He returns my smirk, "Like I'd give you the honor of getting anywhere near my face, darling."

The tip of my tongue comes out as I make a face at him.

"You're so easy to get a reaction out of." He taunts.

I purse my lips, refusing to react instead, saying, "In case you didn't listen to Conrad's instructions, the two of us are supposed to be engaged. So start acting like it."

Conrad gave the order that we pose as a pair of poor springtime fiance's going into a bar, so it would enable us to get the information we needed from the bartender without suspicion from the other patrons.

But both me and Jax know that Conrad just likes seeing us as a couple.

Jax's eyes glint in the sun, "Oh? Am I not being romantic enough for you?"

I don't bother giving him the eye roll he expects.

His grin only widens as he throws his arm over my shoulder, drawing me closer to his hard chest, "Is this better?"

I offer him my sweetest smile, saying through my teeth. "You have five seconds to get your bleeding hands off me before I kill you."

He boops my nose. "You mean attempt to kill. Let's be honest, how far could you really make it?"

I'm about to make him pay for being such a-

"Oh, look, here we are." He interrupts my thoughts, tightening his arm over my shoulder.

"You are a lucky little boy that I didn't cut off your lips for saying that!" I hiss at him right before we enter the dark bar.

He winks at me as we enter, "Glad to know you're thinking about my lips."

The bar is dark and mildewy on the inside. As soon as I enter, I immediately want to get out as quickly as possible.

I notice several sparingly dressed girls making eyes at Jax as we enter. He notices too, and instead of looking away like anybody with a half decent heart would, he winks at them.

"I pity any girl who falls in love with you." I say, sweetly hanging onto his arm as we make our way to the back of the bar where the bartender stands, "If only your attention span was as large as your ego."

"At least I have confidence." He replies back just as sweetly.

I make a face like he's just said something clever. "At what price."

He laughs and shoves my shoulder.

Finally, we reach the bartender, a youngish man with a mustache. I give him a smile I've perfected over the years of not looking too flirty but not uninterested.

"Hello." I don't so much as blink with disgust as the man's eyes crawl all over my body.

He gives me a rotten toothed grin, "What are you here for, little lady?"

Jax frowns beside me, stepping slightly in front of me before giving his usual open smile to the bartender.

I raise an amused eyebrow at him, which he ignores, instead saying in a gruff voice, "We need to talk with you privately."

The bartender's rotten grin disappears and is replaced with an even more foul expression, "So sorry, but I'm working at the moment."

"Oh, I'm so sorry," Jax says, giving him his own inpatient grin, "But I too am working at this moment. And you really don't want to get in the way of my boss."

The bartender frowns even more.

I decide it's time for me to take over. Lowering my voice, I step forward. "I'm so sorry for my fiance's rudeness. But we were told that you know the whereabouts of a certain prince."

The bartender's eyes widen as a sly smile forms on his face,"maybe I do." He shrugs, staring at my chest. "Maybe I don't."

"Isha." Jax growls under his breath.

I ignore him, hardening my expression. "I'm so sorry, but my boss really needs to know." The threat behind my voice is easy to read, but this man obviously doesn't think there's any need to be afraid of me. What a poor mistake to make.

His eyes still cling to my curves, tracing up before he says in a coy voice, "Maybe I'll tell you if you give me the right price."

"That's it." Jax leans over the counter, grabbing a fist full of the man's shirt. "Tell me now where the prince is or Conrad of the Swarm is going to let me kill you."

He's making more of a scene than I would like. But the mere suggestion of Conrad's name makes the man freeze.

The bartender shakes himself, scoffing. "You little liar. You expect me to believe that you two little scumbags are working for the Conrad."

Jax lets his easy grin return, releasing the man. "Alright man don't believe me. But I'd sleep with one eye open tonight if I were you."

The bartender looks at us for a long moment, taking our nice yet simple clothing. The daggers at our sides, the confident way we hold ourselves. Finally, he spits on the counter shaking his head. "Fine." He looks at me again, taking me in for a final time. "But if you tell your bloody boss I took this long, you might wanna watch out, Little lady."

I don't say anything.

Jax shrugs his shoulders. "Touch the little lady," He spits, "and I might come back for you myself."

I'm oddly shocked that Jax cares about what happens to me. But maybe that's what happens when you've known someone as long as the two of us have known each other.

After Jax's little show, we get out of the bar quickly with the concordance of where the young prince lives.

It's been nearly a year of us searching to get this address for Conrad.

Conrad has been plotting the death of The King for nearly twelve years now. And now, finally, we're getting close to Conrad's plan coming to fruition.

Conrad realized years ago that the King's children will inherit the King's place if he ever dies.

So before Conrad plans to kill the King himself, he has to make sure that all four of the King's children die as well, so there's nobody left to inherit the throne when their father dies. Leaving room for Conrad to come to power while the country is in chaos trying to find a new leader.

All of the King's children are over the age of eighteen and are currently living in hiding. After we killed the King's first kid three years ago, the rest of his children went into hiding. We've been searching them down to kill ever since.

We've killed three of them, but didn't know where the fourth was hiding. But now we have the address of his house.

CHAPTER 2

We arrive back at The Swarm just after dusk.

When me and Jax come around the back of the house, Leela, Arad, and Dan are sitting outside the cellar entrance waiting for us.

I give them a curt nod as Jax leaves me to join his other friends.

We've all trained together for years, but I've never really fit in with any of the other teenagers at the Swarm.

I'm about to venture down into the cellar when Jax calls out, "If you ever want to be engaged again your welcome to," he waggles his eyebrows, then winks, "Come hang out."

Mangled laughter from his friends follows his words.

In response, I reach for the dagger at my thigh and throw it behind me, not caring what or who it hits.

The Inside of The Swarm is semi crowded with people.

I try to make my way past all of them without being noticed. I'm almost to my room when Quincy, with her graying black hair, walks into my path.

"How bad of a mission did it have to be to get that look on your face, love?"

I roll my eyes, trying to get past her to my small bedroom, "A successful one with Jax."

She laughs. "Oh come on, you two are friends."

I think of the way he stepped in front of me at the bar. Then think of his last words to me. "No. He's not one of my friends."

Quincy shrugs, "Your loss, dear."

"Ha!" I scoff. "I'm going to go get changed."

I hear Jax and his friends come into the building behind me, their voices all laughter and flirting. I glance over just in time to see Leela swat Jax's shoulder and lean in close. I roll my eyes.

Quincy moves to the side to let me pass when a strong voice I've learned to fear over the years sounds from the entrance to the upstairs.

The voice even makes Jax, Leela, Arad, and Dan shut up.

"Isha, Jax. Come with me."

I turn to see Conrad standing in the upstairs doorway. How he found out me and Jax had already arrived back is a mystery.

Immediately, without thinking, both me and Jax follow him upstairs.

Jax is quite besides me.

"How was your mission?" Conrad asks in a conversational tone.

"Perfect." I say, brightly.

Conrad nods, taking his seat on an expensive couch. He nods to me and says, "Isha, love, go fetch tea from the kitchen."

I nod quickly, rushing away, leaving Jax alone with Conrad.

After I've grabbed the tea, I return to find both of them quiet and looking at me.

I clear my throat. "I hope Jax told you of our success." I say with a bright smile.

Conrad returns it with his own brilliant smile. "He did. We also decided that we'd give you the honor of killing my last obstacle to power."

I choke. "Sorry what?"

Conrad's smile stays firm. "You heard me. I want you to assassinate the last of the king's children for me."

I can still remember the first time I killed someone with absolute clarity. I can still smell the blood. I remember how Conrad had told me killing would get easier with time. But it's been four years since my first kill, and I still dread every assassination I've ever had to perform.

I try to form words to tell him how I don't deserve this honor without getting on his bad side and end up having to put my hands in hot coals as punishment, but before I can form words, Jax cuts in.

"Conrad." He says, "Don't you think Isha might get a little queasy at having to kill such an important gentleman? I think I could do it ten times better."

Both me and Jax flinch as Conrad's smile transforms into a look we both associate with pain. A moment passes in which nothing happens, I release a breath.

Jax's head snaps back. Conrad's fist connects with his jaw. I close my eyes as Conrad says in a light tone to me, "I'm so sorry, Isha, that Jax was trying to steal the gift I'm giving you. I'll make sure he's properly punished for his jealousy."

Jax doesn't so much as flinch at Conrads word. Though his jaw looks raw. Conrad usually only hits us where nobody will notice, I suppose today he forgot.

Guilt crawls under my skin. Jax shouldn't have tried to help me.

I don't meet either of their eyes as I ask Conrad, "When do you want me to leave?"

"Tonight. Why should I wait any longer than I have to save the world? Now, Jax, you will come with me."

Sometimes I wonder how Conrad is any better than the king himself.

CHAPTER 3

I move through Mondan's streets like a sleek black shadow in tight black and forest green clothing, a black mask obscuring my facial features.

The prince is currently hiding in a small manor just outside of the city.

It takes me an hour to get outside of the city gates before I finally reach a large, dark green, three-story house.

I survey the house for a good ten minutes, trying to think through where in the house they would keep an eighteen year old prince they were afraid could be killed at any moment.

The answer was the middle story of the house in the second bedroom on the right.

I climb the outside of the house until I reach the second story window.

Using a lockpicking tool, I open the window in nine seconds.

With quiet steps, I enter the house, shoving down the dread I feel every time before a kill.

Maybe this time it will feel right, like Conrad always says it should.

I take a deep breath, steadying myself as I quietly open the door to the prince's room.

The room is extravagant. To my surprise, there's a little plaque on the inside of the door with the prince's name, Tay Quintell Seer, engraved into metal.

As quietly as I possibly can, I walk up to the bed as I prepare my dagger for a clean blow.

I leap silently up onto the bed frame and-

This can't be right.

I stare in shock.

The prince is supposed to be an eighteen-year-old boy. Not this.... this little boy.

The kid in the bed can't be older than eight.

I stare shocked, at the little boy's dark body and innocent frame, still pudgy with his baby fat.

Conrad wants me to kill this little child.

A child.

I can't take my eyes away from his little body. I've never killed a child before. My blade feels slippery in my sweaty palms.

I choke on my own spit, trying to justify this kill in my head.

Conrad told us all that the King's children were just like their father. Monsters. But how could this little boy be as bad as his father? His mind isn't even fully developed yet.

I can't kill him.

I won't kill this little boy.

In a split second, an idea flies into my mind. It's a crazy, dumb idea. But sometimes I'm a crazy, dumb girl.

All of the Swarm assassins have to keep a small, powered container of nightlock with them in case they get captured.

As quietly as I can, I take the smallest pinch of the nightlock in my fingers just enough to sedate someone for a short amount of time. Then, before I talk myself out of it, I toss the powder in the little boy's mouth in the same movement I snatch him up and leave through his bedroom window.

The second I hit the ground, I drop the little boy onto the grass.

I race back up to his bedroom. Once I get there I pull out my dagger. Steadying my breath I slice my own arm open. Once the blood has pooled out of me, I smear my own blood over the covers.

Hopefully, everybody will think I killed him.

As quickly as I can, I once again race back down to the boy on the ground, throwing him over my shoulder.

And then I run.

I run like it will undo the stupid thing I just did. I run like it will give me the reason I did it. Finally, I stop just outside of town and force myself to slow down and think through reasons and a plan.

Dropping the little boy a little too roughly on the ground I force myself not to panic.

It doesn't work.

Why in the living hell did I just do that!

Why? Why? Why?

But I'm not really asking why. Because the moment I saw this little boy, I saw two futures lay themselves out in front of me.

One where I killed this little boy, Conrad goes to power and uses all of his assassins to kill the people he doesn't like, forever.

But there was also a second future. One where I stood up to Conrad and didn't kill this prince. A future where I might stand up for myself, starting with this little boy.

Because deep down I know Conrad is no better than the king.

So I'm going to stop him.

CHAPTER 4

By the time I get back to The Swarm I've made a huge decision.

I'm going to leave The Swarm.

I'm tired of working for Conrad who is a liar. A cheat. And murder. I'm still not sure what I'm doing. All I know now is that I'm leaving.

I stuff the little prince in a duffel bag under my bed. And try to relax.

Unfortunately for me, the universe has been plotting my downfall for years, and today is the day it's decided to take action.

I try to get a little bit of sleep after I arrive back at The Swarm, but I barely get an hour, due to the fact that I have the little boy I was supposed to kill, half poisoned, and sleeping under my bed.

No stress, right?

To my utter panic after being home for two hours, Conrad barges into my bedroom with a paper under his arm and a snarl on his face concealed behind a smile.

"It says they just found blood on the sheets, no body. What did you do with the body, Isha?"

His eyes flick over me, trying to see if I'm going to confront him about lying to me.

How could I ever let a man who kills children become the king?

I want to kill myself for not coming up with a good excuse to tell Conrad, so I say the first thing that pops into my head.

"I buried it."

For a brief moment, I think Conrad might kill me.

Finally, he says in an even tone, "well then, I'll have to take note of the fact that after years of me taking care of you, you can't even do what I ask."

"And what is that?"

He lets out a cruel laugh, "We always mark the bodies after we kill them, Isha. Remember that?"

He says my name like it's poison.

I know I'll be punished for my words but at this moment I'm more worried that the prince could wake up at any moment and start screaming.

I need to leave tonight.

Conrad can sense fear, Isha. Don't let him.

Making myself smile, I say, "Nice chat."

Against my better judgment, I walk out of my room leaving the prince alone inside with the man who wants him dead.

Conrad leaves a moment after.

Quincy and the others are ecstatic when they read the morning's tragic papers about the missing prince.

I smile and nod, and wonder if they've all killed children before too.

Each time I try to sneak away from the group, somebody begins talking to me. That is, everybody except Jax, who's in and out of the house all day with his group of friends. I notice he walks with a slight limp.

At dinner, which we have upstairs with Conrad, I think I might die wondering if the prince is awake screaming downstairs. Or worse, what if he got out of the bag and is running around down there.

All through dinner, I feel like everybody can tell I have a secret.

I'm relieved when I'm able to go back to my tiny room.

My relief only lasts a second, though, as I realize it's now time for me to make a plan.

The thought overwhelms me so much that I kick the wall, which I immediately regret, not because it hurt my foot but because it might put a hole in the thin walling. Plus, Jax is right next door to me, and I have zero desire to have a hole in the wall connecting our rooms.

I decide I'm going to take things one step at a time.

First I'll pack my bag to leave.

I tear out all of my clothes and a thin traveling pack, trying to work quickly only packing necessities. Halfway through packing I realize something. If I leave tonight, I'm never going to be able to come back to be with these people.

Some I won't miss. But a few others I've grown to love as much as family.

But a normal family doesn't kill to make their leader happy, I remind myself.

"Knock, knock." Jax says the words 'Knock knock' instead of actually just knocking.

I almost jump out of my skin as the door begins opening before I can yell at him to leave me alone.

Frantically, I try to shove my bag under my bed before remembering I have a prince under their and-

"Aces, Isha. What are you doing?" Jax leans against my door judging me.

"I'm, um, going out." I say curtly. "But a better question is, what are you doing in my room?"

He gives me a naughty smile, "Good question."

"Get out before I kill you."

"I thought we already covered the fact that you could only attempt to kill me."

"Get out."

He crosses his arms. "Sure, but first I want to know what you're plotting."

My face pales.

"I'm not plotting anything." My voice doesn't sound convincing, even to my own ears.

His eyes stray around my room. He raises an eyebrow at my clothes everywhere on the ground.

As he speaks, he ticks things off on his fingers, "You've been looking for a way to get away from everyone all day. You were anxious for dinner to end. You did something to make Conrad mad, and now you're packing your bags. It looks and sounds like a plot to me."

"Well, I guess you're just a bad detective, then."

We stare each other down for a long minute before he sighs, looking over my head, "Whatever."

He turns to leave.

"Muf!"

Goodbye life.

My whole body goes on high alert, and it takes everything in me not to look over at the bed where a sound just came from.

Jax's head whips around, cutting around the room, "What was that sound?"

I look at him innocently, "What sound?"

"That-"

"Muf!" The prince cries out again.

"That sound." Jax's voice is accusing as he looks over at the bed, "Isha what's going on I-"

I pounce at him. Simultaneously grabbing Jax's shoulders, slamming the door shut, and finally pinning him to the ground, clamping my hand hard over his mouth.

I get up close to him, glaring, "Don't say a word."

He snatches my wrist, flinging me hard onto my back. For a split second, the air leaves my lungs. Quickly before he can pin me, I flip myself back up, pinning his shoulder's down with my legs.

"Be quiet!" I hiss in a viscous whisper.

"You're the one who attacked me!" He says, too loudly for my taste.

"Be quiet! Please." My last word comes out desperate.

"Isha." His voice holds a warning tone: "What did you do?"

A loud moan comes from under my bed.

His leg shifts under me. Before I can fully understand what's happening, he's lunging towards my bed.

I try to pull him backward, but he turns at the last second, pinning me hard against my dresser.

"Isha. What did you do?" His voice is so low now, I can feel the rumble in his chest as he speaks the words.

A knock sounds at the door.

We both jump, but Jax doesn't let me go.

"What is it?" Jax asks.

Quincy's voice comes from outside, "I heard lots of...banging. Is everything alright in there?"

"Oh, it's just fine." If Quincy could see Jax's face, the words wouldn't have sounded so... suggestive.

"Oh-" Quincy's voice sounds flustered. "It took you long enough-uh ur I mean, sorry. I'll just leave you two to it then."

I give Jax my most loathing glare, even though he did just save us from any sounds we may make.

He sighs. "If I let you go, are you going to attack me again?"

I give him a pleasant smile. "Most definitely. Unless you leave."

"You are completely impossible."

"Too bad."

He gives me another long look before his expression shifts to a serious one I've barely ever seen him wear, "What, or who is under your bed, Isha?"

At the word 'who' his face grows angry again.

I don't respond, instead opting for silence.

"Isha." His voice is still so low that only I can hear it: "I know we've not always gotten along but deep down we're friends and I-" He cuts himself off coughing. "I just want you to know that I don't always agree with Conrad either and I see the way you hate killing for him. You can tell what's happening."

He could be lying to me, then immediately go running to tell Conrad.

But suddenly something deep inside of me snaps- that part of us humans who really can't keep a secret.

"I have the prince under my bed." I say it as bluntly as possible.

Jax just stares at me, "You have the full grown prince, who's supposed to be dead under your tiny bed?"

"No, that's the thing; he's just a little boy. I couldn't kill a little boy, so I half poisoned him so he'd sleep. And now I have to get out of here before he fully wakes up."

To my surprise, Jax releases me from against the dresser, sighing once again, "You're crazy. You know that right?"

This is it, I think, the moment he's going to go tell Conrad I lied to him, and then I'll get killed.

But instead of leaving the room to go to Conrad, he walks over to my bed, pulling out the bag containing the prince before unbuttoning it. He looks down at the prince, who seems to have fallen back asleep.

"Alright then." Jax gives me another dramatic sigh, "You better explain more once we're somewhere safe." With that, he hefts the bag over his shoulder and moves to the door.

"You can't take him out there!" I say, shocked.

He rolls his eyes at me, "And why not?"

Before I can give him one of a million reasons why not, he throws his arm tight over my shoulder, drawing me close against him.

I gasp but I don't say anything as we walk out to find everybody staring at us.

"And where are you going?" Quincy asks us suspiciously.

Jax shrugs, hefting the bag up higher on his shoulder,"places." Then he shoots them a wicked grin."Don't expect us back till morning." With me still pinned against him he practically drags me out of the house.

The moment we get outside I round on him,"was there no better way you could have done that?" I say furiously wishing my face wasn't burning quite so red.

Jax looks down at me with a smirk,"oh their most definitely was."

I'm not quite sure what to say in response to this so I just walk away before I actually do him some permanent damage.

"Um, you're going the wrong direction."

I really hate him.

Without a word I whip around and begin marching in the opposite direction, not bothering to ask him where he's planning on going.

After a moment I hear his feet against the ground behind me.

Once we've walked for about ten minutes in utter silence I can't do it anymore. Not pausing for him I ask over my shoulder,"Why haven't you asked me about it yet."

"I'm a little bit afraid of you at the moment."

I roll my eyes,"well you could at least tell me where I'm going!"

"What if I like watching you pretend to be all independent?"

Why can he make me turn so red with just a small sentence?

"Why are you so impossible!"

"Is that a question or a statement?"

"See, there you do it again!"

"I'm sorry."

I can't lie, I'm a little bit surprised by his apology which leaves me feeling like crap-

"AAAAAA!"

I whip around at the sound.

Jax is already taking the sack of his shoulder and undoing the straps, the little prince inside of the bag is thrashing around.

Jax shoots me a glare as he opens the sack.

Jax's works quickly until the tiny prince is free.

Thank the heavens we're deep in the woods in a clearing where nobody can see us. Maybe Jax isn't all that bad of a partner to have...

Prince Tay's crying quiets as he sits up his frizzy afro of black hair messy.His dark skinned cheeks stained with tears.

The little boy's eyes widen to the size of dinner plates in terror as he looks at the two darkly dressed teenagers in front of him. I regret leaving the daggers strapped to my thighs so out in the open.

"We're umm not going to hurt you." I say in what was supposed to have a comforting effect but has the exact opposite as the little boy begins screaming.

Prince Tay stands as quickly as he can,"Help! Help! Help!"

Even deep in the woods I'm worried that somebody is going to hear the tiny prince.

"We're not going to hurt you? Really?" Jax rolls his eyes at me before he crouches down next to the hysterical prince.

"Hey little man."

"You're the people Nursey told me about!." The prince sobs."The people trying to kill me!"

Jax laughs a little,"we're not trying to kill you I promise."

The boy doesn't look convinced.

I really wish we'd just keep walking to wherever Jax had in mind.

Jax talks quietly for a moment with the boy until to my great surprise Prince Tay laughs before Jax lifts the little boy up onto his shoulders.

The boy actually giggles as Jax begins running with him aboard,"try to keep up!" He calls over his shoulder to me.

I follow behind Jax for a few more minutes until to my surprise a tall tower comes into view.

"Whoa," Prince Tay gasps,"do you live here?"

Jax grins glancing over at me with the proud look of a little boy presenting something,"I wish."

"What is this?" I ask as we approach a cracked wood door that Jax's opens for me.

"Just a place I found years ago and like to hang out." He shrugs with nonchalance that makes me laugh.

We make our way to the top floor of the tower where a light summer breeze blows in through from all sides where painless windows stretch all the way down to the floor showcasing a gorgeous view of the city and forest.

"I can't believe this is where you've been hiding all these years."

"Le'me down!" Tay attempts to jump down from Jax's shoulders.

"Whoa little man, let me help you." He swings Tay down off his broad shoulders, I notice the muscles in his back move through his tight shirt as he does so and wonder what he looks like without-

What the crap.

I don't even attempt to let my mind keep wandering down that path as I tear my eyes away from the cute image of Jax and Tay sitting at one of the tall painless windows as Jax points out the constellations in the sky.

Instead of thinking about how adorable the two of them are together I try to put together what I'm going to tell Jax.

"Um, um, why does she look so like so mad?"

I glance down at Tay who's pointing at me but looking at Jax like he's his hero.

"Because she's stressed out." Jax says, glancing over at me.

I roll my eyes.

"Oh! I know about being stressed out, that's why I've never met daddy. Because he's too stressed out to meet me."

What? The King has never even met his own son?

"You've never met your father?" If this little one really has never met his father then the plan I have hatching in my head is going to work perfectly.

He shakes his head then looks up at Jax admiringly,"I wish you were my daddy."

Jax laughs,"You're a funny little man."

Tay grins a gaped toothed smile looking over at me with notably less admiration,"Then I guess you could be my mommy?"

Jax finds this hilarious, I don't.

All I want to do is debrief with Jax about what's happening but the Jax who seemed wholly interested in my plan an hour ago is now giving all of his soul attention to Tay.

Tay and Jax run around for what feels like hours but in reality is only half of one.

Finally Tay seems a little bit tired and falls down.

"I have a new game."

"Really?" Jax raises his eyebrow.

"Yep. I'm gonna ask you both questions."

"No." I say bluntly.

"She means yes," Jax tells Tay.

"No. I do not." Tay obviously believes Jax not me and begins.

"Are you two in love?"

"Wow you get right to business don't you." Jax laughs though he doesn't look at me.

I roll my eyes.

"Well?" Tay looks at us expectantly.

"No, we are not." I tell him.

Tay looks disappointed,"Well are you friends?"

I find myself looking at Jax for this answer, sure we've known each other our whole lives, and i know more about him than I know about most people, and we've gone on missions together which we have fun on when we aren't fighting but does that make us friends?

"Don't look at me." Jax raises his hand.

I look away down at Tay then say with confidence, mostly because I think it will annoy Jax,"No, we're not friends."

Instead of being annoyed this makes Jax smile from ear to ear, which I find oddly enduring.

Tay gets a wicked little smile,"Are you friends who kiss?"

Jax laughs again, smirking at me,"Not yet."

"That's it." I tell Tay,"I'm done with this game and it's time for you to go to sleep."

"No!" He leaps up running away.

"Give the guy a break he just slept under your dirty bed for a day, he doesn't want to sleep now."

"But I really need to talk to you!" I remind him.

Jax shrugs his shoulders which I'm still trying not to notice,"Whatever, he can listen if he wants."

"But what I'm going to tell you is not for little ears to hear about."

"He's not even going to be listening to us."

"He might." I argue.

Jax gives a pointed look over to where Tay is laying on his belly watching a little marry bug waddle on the ground.

"Yeah he's really just dying to listen to you," Jax drawls

"Fine." I grump, "But you better be listening because I'm only saying this once."

Jax sits up, crosses his legs and puts his hands in his lap smiling stupidly, "Fine I'll be a good little boy."

I snort.

I take a moment to try to put together my thoughts before finally beginning in a hushed tone, "Alright basically I'm done killing for Conrad."

"I know." Jax interrupts which would have been annoying if I wasn't such a curious answer.

"How do you know?" I give him a skeptic look.

"You've always hated killing. Why do you think I volunteered to go kill the prince for you? I know you hate it." Oddly I'm touched by this, but before I can read too much into it I clear my throat,"well ummm anyways. When I went to kill him," My eyes drift over to Tay now dancing in the moonlight,"I thought he was older but I just couldn't bring myself to kill a little boy."

Jax nods but to my surprise doesn't interrupt.

"Without thinking I kidnapped him instead."

Jax sighs,"Is this you trying to tell me you have no plan."

I shut him up with a glare,"No, I have a plan! And it's a good one," I add.

"Alright then tell me this great plan." He accompanies his words with air quotation marks.

I huff,"we're going to kill the King still pretending to work for Conrad than before Conrad can take control by saying the throne has no heirs we'll step in and put Tay on the throne and chose a really great counselors for him that will teach him how to rule justly, unlike his father and unlike Conrad would have ruled." I finish trying to pretend like my plan has no loopholes in it.

Jax just stares at me.

He sighs,"I have to give it to you. You're brave as heck."

I deflate a little feeling oddly like crying,"Look!" I say forcing anger so I don't cry, "I know it's a bad plan! But I can't just let Conrad become king then just use us all of us at the Swarm to kill all of the people he doesn't like!"

For a second I think Jax might get mad right back at me but instead he nods,"okay. Calm down, your plan isn't that bad, it just needs more time. I think it will work." He offers a comforting smile, "besides you won't be able to mess up if I help you."

I stare at him shaking my head."Why are you just helping me?"

"Why can't I just be a good person in your eye's for once?" Jax asks me, looking at me like my small question really hurt him.

"I-I'm sorry I never said you were a bad person."

"Yeah whatever." He stands up glancing over at Tay who's already fallen asleep again; the drug I gave him is still not fully worn off.

Jax scoops Tay up, placing him down against the arch of a window, before he walks back over to me smirking down at me, all traces of hurt gone from his face.

"You know you need a haircut."

"My hair is none of your business!" I gasp, whacking him on the shoulder as he sits down next to me.

"Remember when you first came to live in the Swarm and you had no hair?" He laughs at the memory.

"Shut up! I had hair!" I had been living on the streets before I came to live in the Swarm and had needed to steal for my meals. So I had cut off my hair so shopkeeper's wouldn't grab me by my hair when I was running from them.

I chuckle, "I did look pretty bad, didn't I?"

"I can't agree to that without you attempting to kill me." He says.

"You're getting smarter."

Suddenly out of the blue his voice changes, "why aren't we friends?"

I glance at him to find his eye's tracing the stars from outside the windows.

I look away, "I don't know. You've never seemed to like me."

He gives a ruff laugh, "I do like you."

An awkward silence passes between us.

I clear my throat, "we don't know that much about each other."

"Liar. We've lived with each other for years."

"Well we don't know normal things about each other."

"Like what?"

I search my brain,"like um..." Heck. How do I know this much crap about Jax? "Like, I don't even know your...um... your favorite color."

"Forest green."

"What?"

"That's my favorite color, forest green."

"Oh."

"I've decided something." Jax sit's up,"I want to know all of your favorites."

"What?" I roll my eyes.

"Tell me all of your favorite things and I'll tell you mine."

I laugh, shaking my head,"fine. Ask me whatever you want."

"Favorite food?"

"Apples." I say.

"That's a stupid favorite food." His nose wrinkles.

"I'm done with this game if you're going to be rude."

He raises his hands,"sorry, it's just... apples are such a boring food."

"Well maybe I'm a boring person."

He laughs,"I know that's not true."

I roll my eyes,"Alright your turn."

We talk for an hour just going back and forth until finally I yawn.

"Am I boring you that much?" Jax's eyes sparkle.

"Well Jax," I say, the snap returning to my voice. "Maybe I've just had a long day and am tired."

His wicked grin returns,"then you should go to sleep. I'll be right here if you need to cuddle."

My jaw drops,"there's a child right there Jax!"

His grin widens,"does that mean you want to cuddle?"

I get close to his face,"remember I have two daggers strapped to my thigh, so I wouldn't say another word if I were you."

"Are you trying to get me to touch your thigh?"

In a quick movement I pull my dagger out pressing it hard against his skin.

I feel a laugh boiling in his throat,"is this supposed to be threatening? Because you look really cute trying to be fierce."

I gasp suddenly, also trying very hard not to laugh,"you are impossible."

After another moment of the dagger against his throat I drop it from his neck sighing and moving to the other side of Tay.

"Good night." He says in a sing-song voice as I make myself comfortable on the ground.

"Screw you." I say in response.

I fell asleep to his laughter.

CHAPTER 5

I wake to the sun glaring down on me and a warm summer breeze coming in through the windows.

The windows.... Where the crap am I!

I sit up panicked, heart racing before my brain finally catches the rest of my body.

Yesterday's events come back to me in a blur.

Shuddering I look to my side where Tay and Jax had been sleeping only to see neither of them there.

The panic comes back full force.

A quick survey of the room shows neither Jax nor Tay are up here in the tower.

My heart stops, wondering if Conrad somehow saw us all up in the tower last night.

I jump to my feet. Yanking on my boots I run to the stairway leading out of the tower when all of a sudden I hear jolly voices coming from below.

I blink twice before cautiously making my way down the stairs.

The voices get louder the father down I get until I see a small door I didn't notice last night.

Slowly I push the door open just a bit wary of a trap. It's darker in this room and it takes me a moment for my eyes to adjust.

"YOU SCARED ME HALF TO DEATH!"

Both Tay and Jax just about just jump right out of their skin wiping around to see me in the doorway.

Jax shoots me a grin,"at least we only scared you half to death not all the way."

I shake my head."You know I thought that Conrad had come for you guys!"

Jax's smile remains,"we both know he would have taken you not me if he'd come for us."

"Who's Conrad?" Tay asks from where he's sitting on a small bed in the corner of the room.

Now that my rage has calmed down I take in the rest of the room, it's small and simple with a few boxes in the corner next to a bed.

"He's nobody you need to worry about." Jax says, turning to Tay.

Tay, content with this, runs over to the boxes in the corner and fishes out a loaf of bread from one before running back to me offering it up.

"When I'm grumpy Nursery says I need to eat."

"So wise for such a young man, you really know how to make the ladies swoon by offering them food." Jax's smile somehow only grows bigger.

I try not to scowl as I take the bread,"I'm not grumpy, I'm just stressed out."

Plopping down on the ground I look over at the boxes,"how come there's food down here?" I ask Jax.

He shrugs,"sometimes I like to spend the night here."

I don't push him further on the topic.

We make our way upstairs after we all eat breakfast.

"So my lady what's the plan for the day?" Jax yells over his shoulder as he chases Tay up the stairs.

I smile despite myself then frown because I have no idea what we're going to do now.

"I-I'm not sure..." I stutter.

Jax stops at the top of the stairs only slightly out of breath,"well I take it we can't really bring Tay over to the Swarm with us unless we both want to face Conrad's impending doom?"

I raise an eyebrow,"Impending doom?"

"I like the dramatic."

"I'm bored!"

We both look over at Tay.

I open my mouth to tell him we're busy saving his sorry life but before I get the words out Jax says,"I have a chess board downstairs in that room we were just in. If you go get it I'll teach you how to play."

Without a word Tay leaps down out of the room.

"What a cute kid."

"Yeah, yeah," I shrug my mind occupied."One of us is going to have to go back to the Swarm and say the other person is sick or something, we can't just leave Tay here by himself..."

"Okay you go back and I'll hang out with my new little friend."

"What if they ask questions about where I've been all night."

He laughs,"I already told them not to expect us back till morning."

I roll my eyes,"nobody is going to believe we spent the night together."

Jax shrugs,"people are more dumb than you think."

"Fine but if Leela tries to kill me when I get there it's your fault."

He cocks his head,"why would Leela try to kill you?"

I almost laugh. How in the world can he not tell Leela has been obsessed with him for years? Instead of informing him that Leela has been in love with him for years I just wave it away,"no reason."

In return I get a funny look from him.

"Alright I'm leaving." I say as Tay comes bonding up the stairs chess board in toe.

"Bye Isha," Jax waves his hand,"have a beautiful, beautiful girl."

Tay grins in the same way as Jax,"bye Ishy! Have a beautiful girl!"

I laugh giving them both a look,"you're both doomed."

I only get semi lost on my way to the Swarm house.

Finally I get their smiling like an idiot as I throw open the cellar door.

All the commotion in the room stops as all eyes stick to me like glue.

"Um hi guys..." I say, awkwardly stepping into the room.

Glancing over at a corner I see Leela with her friends glaring at me. I give her my nicest smile which she returns with a gesture that heavily leans on the middle finger.

I sigh walking into the room seeing a long day ahead of me.

Quincy finds me in my room an hour later. I'm thinking through a plan for what me and Jax are going to do.

"Ahem?"

My eyes shoot up from starting at the wall to where Quincy stands in my doorway.

I force a smile,"Hi."

Quincy gives me a look, her dark skin creasing,"so you and Jax were.... gone last night."

She's not asking a question. But then she smiles,"tell me about it."

I gulp because there is nothing to say. So I do what I always do and harden my expression,"I don't see how it's any of your business?"

Quincy looks hurt for a moment then shrugs looking at me like I've just disappointed her.

If there's anyone in the world I don't want thinking badly about me it's Quincy. I can deal with Leela and Jax and Conrad, but not Quincy.

I know she can tell something is not quite right,"where is he now?"

"Um he's not feeling very well..."

I can't explain to her what's happened.

I can't tell her any of it. Because as much as I love and adore Quincy, I don't really trust anyone in this god for-saken house.

"I didn't realize you felt the same way about Jax."

"What's that supposed to mean?"

She opens her mouth to respond then shakes her head sighing,"Conrad has called us upstairs in an hour," she glances at my clothing, which are the same clothes I was wearing yesterday."Maybe you should go get changed too."

An hour later the twenty of us who live here at the Swarm are upstairs at Conrad's dining table.

He smiles at us all.

"I've decided we are going to siege the palace in four days time." He waits expectantly so we all clap not knowing what else to do.

He continues,"I would move forward sooner but I'm calling upon my other gangs in different parts of the country to come meet here so we can use them to attack the palace after I assassinate the King."

More polite clapping.

Conrad smiles pleased,"I'll be a king soon, and all of you will be right at my side."

I spend the rest of the day avoiding Leela and her friends while not looking Quincy in the eyes.

Finally I mutter half under my breath to Quincy that I'm going to leave again for the night.

She doesn't say anything as I walk away.

Just before I leave the through cellar the thought strikes me that I should probably go and get some clothes for Jax to change into.

I pause in front of Jax's bedroom door. It's been years since I've been in his small room even though it's right next to mine.

I feel like an intruder as I push open his door.

His room is the same size as mine except much messier with the bed unmade and clothes strewn across the floor. On the small untidy night stand next to his bed there's a journal lying open. Ignoring the surprise I feel at thinking of him writing in the journal each night I open up his dresser.

It feels even more invasive to open up his drawer and grab some clothes for him. I do it anyway, quickly grabbing the first shirt and pants I see. My eyes catch on a piece of paper shoved in the corner of the drawer.

I know I shouldn't look at the paper but curiosity takes over me. Before I can stop myself I snatch the paper.

The paper turns out to be a photograph.

I stare at the beautiful man and woman in the photo for a long time. Finally I put the photo back.

As quickly as I can I leave the room.

It takes me a little bit of wandering and constant checking behind my shoulder to make sure I'm not being followed before I finally find my way to the tower.

In the setting sun with the warm summer breeze blowing through the trees musing the dark green grass, the ancient tower looks beautiful. The scene before me makes me smile as I climb up the stairs to the top floor.

On my up this time I hear noise coming from the small room where we ate our breakfast this morning.

Pushing open the door I find Tay whooshing around the room playing games in his head.

He looks up in surprise, "Ishy!" He shouts with joy running to me and giving me a hug.

I smile down at him loving the way his little arms wrap around my thighs.

"How was your day?" I ask, trying not to feel the normal awkwardness I feel around young children.

He frowns."It was boring because Jax said we couldn't weave the tower, so I just was like so bored but we did make good food and play games!"

"Oh, that um sounds fun ....Do you want to come upstairs with me?"

His little nose wrinkles in distaste,"no! I want to play down here."

His passion makes me laugh,"okay, calm down."

I leave him down in the room and walk up the stairs entering the top of the tower.

In the doorway I pause.

Jax is lying on his side, his white shirt unbuttoned all the way down showing his tanned chest, he's biting the corner of his lip as he plays a game of chess against himself.

For a moment all I do is stare at him and the way the setting sun bounces off of him and pours through his golden hair as his brown eye chart chess pieces.

He glances up.

For a split second our eye's lock.

Jax's grin is infectious and slightly mischievous. He falls onto his back, eyes twinkling,"I know I look sexy down here don't I?"

He does acutely.

"Why can't you be normal for five whole seconds?"

"I was just born too lovable to be normal I suppose."

"Oh poor you." I say, crouching down next to his game of chess," you do know how pathetic it looks for you to be playing this all by yourself don't you?"

"Awww are you feeling jealous that I didn't ask you to play with me?"

"No."

"Don't worry you can play, just be prepared for me to beat the living crap out of you."

I raise an eyebrow, "In your dreams lover boy."

He raises his eyebrow too. "Lover boy?"

"Because you said you were so lovable."

He laughs as I move my first chess piece.

He moves his piece.

My mind wanders to the photo I found in his room earlier.

"I found something in your room today..."

"You miss me that much, huh?" He glances up with amusement, "Did you take a little nap on my bed to feel close to me, too? "

I roll my eyes, "No! I was getting you clothes and I found a picture."

His whole demeanor pauses. Slowly his drift to mine, "What do you mean?"

"I mean I found a picture." I don't know why I'm bringing this up. "It was a man and a woman."

For a long time Jax doesn't say anything. After a long second though he finally nods before saying very quickly, "They're my parents." He doesn't meet my eyes.

"Oh." I can tell I've stepped into a hard topic for him, but for some reason I can't let it go, "What... happened to them?"

He glances away from me then shrugs. "They were performers. Didn't want a kid. They always dreamed of moving down to the coast but were too poor." He runs a hand through his hair, "They, um, heard that there was a gang leader who would take homeless kids. So one day I came home to an empty house and a note with the address of the Swarm." He lets out a hard laugh, "I haven't seen them since."

I feel a sort of longing to reach out and touch his shoulder but I keep it inside.

"I'm sorry." Because what else can you say to a story like that.

Once again Jax shrugs with a smile that doesn't reach his eyes, "You don't need to be sorry, everyone at the Swarm has some sort of pity story."

"I know... but yours is just, really sad."

He looks up at me grinning , "You're really doing a good job of making me feel pathetic right now."

"I'm not trying to make you feel pathetic."

He snorts, "It's your turn Isha."

I ignore him, "I lived with my uncle until I was 12 but he kicked me out after he got remarried."

"Well then, we're quite the pair my lady." He says, reaching across and moving my chess piece for me, "Two abandoned kids from the streets. Unloved and uncared for, destined to find each other." He rolls onto his back laughing.

"Hey!" I slap his hand away and move it myself. "Our backstories aren't a funny topic."

He grins up from the ground, "If you can laugh about something instead of crying, you better choose to laugh."

I smile, "Your turn."

Once again he moves his piece.

We stay like that for a long time just playing chess.

As we do I feel something happening in my body that I'm not used to. A feeling that I want to get closer to Jax, pull him against me and- and what? Jax doesn't have feelings for me and I don't have feelings for him. So where was I going with that stupid thought?

I wasn't going anywhere with it, that's what.

At least that's what I tell myself until it becomes too late for me to think clearly.

CHAPTER 6

The next morning I take the longer path back to the Swarm for no particular reason.

The street to get back to the Swarm is crowded with people I don't recognize briskly walking in all directions. To my fascination every once in a while a person walking down the street will discreetly slip into the yard of the Swarm house.

Feeling rather uneasy I slip unnoticed through the front yard to the back of the house where to my shock the strangers I just barely saw come back here are being let quietly into the basement, through the cellar door.

Kent is the man letting all of the people in, he sees me and offers up a smile as he lets me in behind the strangers.

The basement is hot. Full of the extra body's of people I don't know.

Frowning I push my way through the crowd until I finally find a person I recognize.

Unfortunately it's Leela.

"What's going on?"

Leela's head snaps up at my words, and seeing my face her whole demeanor darkens,"there the people from Conrad's other gangs, duh. They're going to help us with the attack, remember?"

My face darkens too,"if I had remembered I wouldn't have asked you...duh."

Her eyes flick up and down the length of my body,"obviously."

She shoots me a tight lipped smile,"now get out of my way."

She pushes past me and I glower.

All day people arrive.

All day the basement gets hotter and smellier and louder.

At noon I try to go into my room only to find strangers sitting on my dresser looking through my clothes and sitting on my bed.

They're all my age but dressed in the styles of the small towns up north.

One of the boys glances up at me, "do ya want somth'in?" He has a northern drawl.

"Why are you in my room?" My voice comes out with an edge.

He shrugs, "there wasn't much space to be out there. I reckon we have as much right to this room as ya."

I bite down hard on my lip forcing a smile,"well no actually. Because this is my room. So get out. Please."

He looks up at me."and what makes you so special that you feel you have the right to this room?"

"Because it's mine you-"

"Is there a problem dear?"

Everyone in the room goes quiet and I watch the young man's eyes whip to the man standing behind me. I don't even need to turn around to tell it's Conrad.

Slowly I turn around shaking my head,"no sir."

"Really, your voice did sound rather...heated."

"I was just asking this man to get out of my room."

Conrad's eyes flash and the young man literally cowers,"get out now. All of you." His voice contains so much steel that the boy doesn't bother to remain any longer, not waiting for any of his friends.

Soon the room is empty.

I should be grateful for the quiet but with Conrad's predatory eyes stalking me it's hard to relax.

"Would you like anything?" I ask my voice barely a whisper.

"Yes, in fact." He smiles all the edges,"I want you to come with me to kill the King when the time comes."

My heart sinks wondering how this will affect what me and Jax plan to do. But there is no use in fighting.

"Alright."

"And?"

It takes me a moment to figure out what he's asking.

Finally it hits me,"thank you for this honor."

"Anytime."

The rest of the day is followed with more self righteous people, being shoved, and pissed off.

When I finally think that my breaking point has come, Quincy finds me.

She takes one good look at me and raises her eyebrow," darlin, for the safety of everyone here I think you might want to call it a night."

I roll back my shoulders,"no, I can stay. I just don't understand why everyone from all of the other gangs are so conceited and-"

Quincy raises a hand to shut me up,"I suppose Jax is still sick?"

My eyes drop to the ground,"umm yeah."

I know she doesn't believe me but she doesn't push it either,"alright then, why don't you go check on him for the night to make sure he's doing alright, huh?"

I'm stuck with the urge to give her a hug but I ignore it,"okay. I'll see you tomorrow."

With a hand on her hip she gives me a nod,"don't stay up too late, and I'll try an get those no good slugs out of your bedroom again."

"Thanks."

"Love ya sweetie."

All I can give her in return is a smile.

Since it was burning hot in the basement I'm surprised to find the sky low and overcast when I get outside.

By the time the tower is within my vision it's raining so hard I can barely see anything.

I race up to the top room expecting a warm room only to remember all the painless floor to ceiling windows.

Both Jax and Tay are racing about the room picking up the blankets and pillows we've been sleeping on.

"Ishy help!" Tay screams at the top of his lungs in real despair as he tries to pile all of the small pillows in his tiny arms.

Jax even in the midst of a storm smiles at the little boy as though the world isn't a rushed thing, he glances to see me in the doorway as he takes one of the pillows from Tay, he gifts me with a smile too.

It's funny how I think of smiles as gifts, only given when truly deserved. While Jax on the other hand seems to give out smiles as if they don't change the directory of the sun. As if one smile from him doesn't fill everybody who sees it with light, as if it cost him nothing. But I suppose a smile coasting you nothing is normal... I wonder if my smile makes anyone else be filled with light?

CHAPTER 7

Jax P.O.V.

The rain is pouring over our heads.

"Where are we gonna go?" Isha has to shout to be heard over the wind and rain rushing in through the painless windows. Her clothes are already soaked making every inch of the fabric stick to her body clinging to her curves, quickly I avert my eyes.

Tay is running around our feet holding my chess board and a blanket half panicked and half exhilarated. The little guy makes me smile every time I look at him.

Still not feeling like my mind won't play dirty tricks on me if I look at Isha, I say in her general direction,"downstairs I guess."

It's the only place I can think of because it has no windows and it should be warm enough for us to wait out the storm.

Without waiting for me to say more Isha snatches Tay's hand racing down the stairs not looking back.

I stand at the top of the stairs for a moment longer just watching the two of them race down the stairs feeling a grin find its way to my face.

Just before Isha throws herself into the downstairs room right behind Tay she throws a glance up the stairs, just for a moment our eyes meet. Her hair soaking wet is plastered to her face and as her eyes meet mine seeing my grin her whole face lights up with a matching smile. For no reason at all I laugh. Then a miracle happens, she laughs too.

She yells something into the room. A moment later Tay appears looking up at Isha, he's smiling too, as she looks back up at me,"get down here!" She yells.

The two of us don't say anything once I reach the two of them at the bottom of the stairs. Then just reading each other's mind the three of us half run, half slip down the stairs until we reach the bottom practically falling out onto the wet grass.

Out here the rain is ten times harder.

"We probably shouldn't have Tay out here!" Isha shouts to be heard over the wind and rain.

"Yeah probably!"

Isha laughs again,"well who gives a crap? We're the only ones out here in this rain!"

Tays already run off splashing in puddles.

I turn to Isha bowing,"my lady? May I have this dance."

I expect her to roll her eyes and walk away but as it turns out only part of that is true because after her eyes roll she grabs my arm and we dance in the rain.

Her hair whips into my face and my arms throw her out dipping her low.

I'm not quite sure when Isha stopped being just the annoying little girl I had to train with to someone I realized I cared about. I think it was just a gradual thing. I didn't just wake up one day realizing that I cared for Isha in more than a 'friend' way and in more than a 'brotherly' way (though the overprotective instincts of a brother were definitely there). It was a more gradual thing until this year when I realized that somewhere in the last four and a half years, Isha meant so much to me that it hurt not to be able to tell her how I felt.

The only person I've ever told about how I feel for Isha is Quincy who over the past few months has listened to my rants about how I know Isha will never love me back.

I'm pathetic, believe me I know.

I also know she doesn't feel the same way about me. And I know I don't deserve her. But if the only way I can get Isha to talk to me is by the two of us fighting I'll do it. And if the only way I can do anything for her is by offering to take her assassination jobs that Conrad gives her then I'll do it. Even if it means facing Conrad's wrath. And even though the two of us have been through so much pressure for the past week, in its own way it's been my own sort of nirvana.

Isha lets go of me.

I stumble into a run as she races for Tay.

"Ha!" I shout snatching Tay up into my arms, he screams with delight.

Suddenly a boom of thunder sounds so hard that it shakes the trees to their roots followed by a moment of silence before a streak of lightning cracks down on the earth.

Me and Isha make eye contact.

"I believe that's our sign to leave, my lady."

"I think you might be right."

Without another word we make our way back up the tower steps, rain still pouring down the stairs.

I hold the door open to the small extra room for Isha and Tay.

Isha pauses inside the room and a moment later I see why.

I had thought that there were no windows in this room. But as it turns out I forgot there's a small little window with bars near the ground that's letting in rain water that is leaving a two inch pile of moving water coating the floor. All of this makes the only true dry place in the room, the bed.

I place an easy smile on my face watching Tay race to the bed making his little body comfortable.

Turning to Isha, the smile is still firm in its place though my heart is pounding in my chest so loud I wouldn't be surprised if she could hear it, I open my mouth making sure to keep any teasing out of my tone,"if you don't feel comfortable sharing the bed, I can try to sleep on the floor."

Literally nothing sounds worse than trying to sleep on the wet ground.

But even if I am an assassin, I'm still a gentleman.

Isha throws me a look, that makes me want to laugh.

"Don't be stupid. We both know you're too much of a wimp to sleep on the wet ground all night. So get on that bed before I make you."

Man, I wish she was saying those words to me in a different situation.

She crosses the room, throws herself onto the bed on one side of Tay and promptly pulls him close to keep him warm.

Taking my time I grab three apples and walk over to the bed.

I can do this.

Spend the night next to Isha.

Spend seven or six hours next to Isha all night.

I can do it and not touch her.

Because I am a gentleman.

I repeat the phrase, I am a gentleman, as I take my spot on the other side of Tay.

A long moment passes just the three of us on the bed.

"Ummm are you going to eat all of those or are you going to share?" Isha points at the apples.

I grin and this time it's easy.

"Oh, these? I was planning on eating them all, but I'd be willing to share if someone asks nicely."

It's too dark in this little room to see her face properly but I know her well enough to imagine the eye roll.

Suddenly I feel a hand smack mine and before I can do anything Isha is chopping into her apple.

"You really have a way with words my darling." I laugh.

"Don't call me your darling."

"All right, my love."

I hear her eyes roll without seeing them.

"You want an apple little man?" I look down to give Tay his food only to see the kids passed out in the space in between our two larger bodies.

Suddenly the reality of it really just being the two of us on this bed hits me. My whole body grows slightly sweaty.

An awkwardness I'm not used to with Isha comes in between us.

Just the two of our breaths filling the silence.

"We need to make a plan." Her voice sounds odd.

"Yeah alright we have a day till Conrad storms the palace." I'm grateful for her talking.

"Right," she says, her voice sounding itself again, "so we need to somehow get Tay back on the throne and find a counselor who will be able to take care of him till he's old enough to rule." Her weight shifts next to me and I try not to memorize the feeling of her so close to me.

She thinks for a moment before she says solemnly ,"Conrad asked me- told me that I'm going to go kill the King with him."

"Isha-." I know how much she hates killing. I want to reach out and comfort her but if I touch her I'm not sure I'll be able to stop.

"It's okay... but," she pauses then says too quickly, "we need to stop Conrad after he kills the king, Jax. We're going to have to kill Conrad. He's not going to stop just because we have the heir to the throne. "

I freeze for a long moment, "If we kill him, how are we going to make sure the other gang leaders don't immediately step forward and take his place?" I ask.

"We're going to have to kill him somewhere public so that the people know there's a new heir and won't let another leader take the throne." She muses.

"What about after he gives his speech to the people about him being their new king?" I offer.

"How are we going to know if he'll give a speech?"

"It's Conrad Isha, if he wins and takes down the King then he's going to rub it in."

"So... when he gives his speech after taking the crown then we're going to have to kill him in front of everyone."

Her body weight shifts besides me. I need to touch her. "Then before the Swarm can regroup. We bring forward Tay to give the people hope and hopefully show the rest of the Swarm members that they can't win, and we peacefully crown Tay and find him a trustworthy person to help counsel him until he can fully take care of the country."

I laugh into the dark, "You make all that sound like a walk in the park, my lady."

She laughs too, "We can do this..."

"Say that again and pretend that you mean it."

"Shut up."

"Say it again, I dare you."

"Fine. We can do this! Happy now?"

"Very."

She sighs, "I'll have to go early to attack the palace and kill the King." Her voice quivers at this and I remind myself to keep my hands to myself,"but you can bring Tay to the palace after the attack."

"I would take your place killing the king in a minute, Isha," I whisper, "I wish you didn't have to kill again."

"You hate killing too." She whispers back.

I love you more.

"I can deal with it." My voice comes out low.

"Thank you, Jax... for- for doing this all with me."

"Don't worry about it."

With that we both fall back into silence but this time it's comfortable.

So comfortable in fact that I have to remind myself once again that I'm a gentleman.

CHAPTER 8

The next day dawns bright and lovely.

How is it that anticipation for something is so much worse than the actual event? All day my mind won't focus and once again I leave the Swarm house early.

I can tell Jax feels the same worry I do, but he's keeping it together better than me playing with Tay when he asks, letting me sit by myself trying to read a romance novel I brought from the Swarm.

I'm not usually one for not eating but my heart is so scared for the next day that Jax practically feeds me like a child before I go off to bed early.

I wake up the next morning beside Jax with Tay between us.

Today's the day.

I might truly die this afternoon. Refusing to think of this I work through the plan instead..

I go back to the Swarm saying Jax will arrive a bit late to the siege on the palace. Screw what teasing I'll go through for it, then later Jax will come back to the house with Tay in a bag.

Then I will leave with Conrad.

Jax will smuggle Tay to the castle then after I kill the King and Conrad goes to take the throne. Then during Conrad's speech, Jax will kill him in front of everyone. I can't even think of it. I will then bring out Tay and give a speech about how everybody must work together to help us crown a new king who we can raise to be the best king we've ever had! Everybody will cheer and everything will be perfect!

I know our plan will never work out that perfectly. Lives are going to be lost today. Nothing is going to end perfectly. Nothing.

Besides me Jax stirs.

I glance over at him to find his eyes open watching me, I give him a half hearted small smile.

"Are you nervous?" I ask.

"I'd be worried if I wasn't."

"What if it doesn't work, and we die?"

"Wow, pessimistic much?" Jax laughs before softening his expression at the anxiety showing itself on my face,"we'll be free either way, I guess. Besides, I'd rather die a hero than live being a villain."

"You stole that quote from something didn't you?"

"Isha, you can't expect me to be this perfect and still be able to make up poetic words for you."

I shake my head. Suddenly my voice cracks,"Jax. We're doing the right thing right?"

"Don't look at me, I'm probably the worst person to ask for advice." He says softly.

"I already knew that,"

We both grin until suddenly there's an odd silence between us and my body gets a small tingle as our eyes stay locked on each other.

Out of the blue a crazy inappropriately timed thought comes to me, Jax wants to kiss me.

I cough trying to pretend I didn't feel whatever just happened."I should get going."

Jax just blinks as I stand to go.

As I reach the stairs his voice hits me,"hey."

I turn,"yeah?"

"Even if you're not my friend, I'm yours." He grins. "Now go show Conrad who Isha really is."

The second I reach the Swarm I barely have any time before Conrad and the other leaders of the smaller gangs usher everyone on the mission out of the house.

As I exit the Swarm it suddenly strikes me that this most likely is the last time I will ever step foot inside this house. Even after all of my years of living here and the killing and torture I've done within these walls it still hurts a little leaving it.

I turn and try not to look back.

We reach the border of the woods within an hour.

Conrad's plan is in its own way rather ingenious. It works in waves, we send out group one to take down the first line of defense around the castle before moving to group two which takes down the next line of defense and so on.

Me and Conrad are the last group who will go in to kill the president. After his death the castle will be in chaos and we will all siege it, taking full power of the kingdom of Mandon.

"Isha."

I jump at the sound of His voice.

I don't look up into Conrad's eyes,"yes?"

His voice is toned with a shade of darkness hidden behind the light,"I realize I've never told you that I'm so proud of you for killing the prince."

My first thought is that Conrad knows.

But no. It's impossible for him to know. Unless...Jax told him something....but no. I won't think badly of Jax... As it turns out he's different then I thought he was all of these years.

If Conrad knew he would have said something.

"Thank you."

His sparkling smile returns as he looks away from me turning to everybody else,"are you ready!" He shouts.

We all nod and some people cheer.

Conrad smiles looking like a predator, who's world is made of prey.

As I sit and wait for Conrad to give me the sign for us to go, I can already feel the familiar shame that I experience before and after every assassination. By this point the feeling is common but never loses its unpleasantness. No doubt Conrad will make me give the King a bit of torture before I kill him.

At least this will hopefully be my last kill.

Nobody is looking or paying attention to me in the slightest, which might have something to do with the fact that I'm sweating so profusely I must smell terrible.

To keep myself from stressing about the rest of the day I force myself to think of something else.

To my surprise a handsome smirking blonde haired boy comes to mind.

I don't let myself wonder why Jax is the first face that came to my mind. I don't let myself think of him playing with Tay, or even just him and me playing our games after Tay falls asleep.

I shake myself away from these weird thoughts I'm having.

Unfortunately my mind hates me and before I could tell it not to, it comes up with the picture of him with his shirt unbuttoned playing chess by himself and...

Suddenly just as the second group goes out I'm staring at not the Jax of my imagination but the very real version of Jax is standing in front of me looking a little bit guilty.

Something must have happened, why else would Jax be here? Where is Tay? What if something happened to Tay! What if... What if....

"Nice of you to join us Jax." Conrad says Jax's name like a curse word, as I'm still trying to figure out what in the bleeding heck he's doing here when he's not supposed to show up until Conrad is moving in to tell the people that he's here to take the crown.

Jax shoots me his most lovely grin.

I attempt not to glare at him.

"Hey, old man." Jax lifts a hand to Conrad, who does not appear to enjoy being referred to as 'old man'.

"You're not supposed to be here." Conrad says his voice is full of knives.

Me and Conrad are on the same page.

Jax shrugs,"I thought I'd help out. I've been here longer than her haven't I?"

It's like he's trying to get on Conrad's bad side.

After a long look Conrad gives him an even smirk,"where have you been all week?"

He knows I've been gone too, he suspects something. He knows Jax will deny being with me.

"I've been with Isha." He says almost proudly.

I guess I was wrong.

If Conrad is surprised by Jax's honesty he doesn't show it,"and what have you and Isha been doing on your little playdates?"

Jax smirks again,"what do you think too lovely people do at night?" He throws an arm over my shoulder.

Do not murder him, Isha. Do. Not. Murder. Him.

Conrad smiles,"then kiss her. I'd love to see your new found affection for each other"

"What?" I choke.

Conrad grins, he knows that even just a week ago i would've killed Jax if he got his face anywhere near mine, he doesn't think I'd kiss him.

"Alright then." Jax says like this is simply a matter of business to attend to.

He swoops his head down closer to mine than without giving me a second of notice his mouth is pressed against mine.

I wait for him to pull away but he doesn't.... Instead letting one of his arms wrap around my back, pulling me tightly against him. His other hand wraps around my hip squeezing it tightly as he kisses me. I'm so frozen I do absolutely nothing but stand with him kissing me, like he acutely means it. Suddenly his body freezes and for a split second he holds me tighter he thumb digging into the delicate skin on the inside of my hip as if it's a hard effort for him to not let his hands begin exploring my body, for him not to press me against a tree and never let me go, all of this last only a second, before he let's me go.

I'm not sure what just happened. I blink at him and he looks just as dazed as I do, but only for a second because then his smirk is back and he bops me on the nose.

"Great acting, you almost made it seem like you like me just a little bit." He glances over to where Conrad used to stand but must have walked away somewhere in the kiss.

I shake myself out of this weird daze,"can we just not talk about what just happened?" I say mostly to myself.

Jax rolls his eyes,"as you wish.

Suddenly I'm knocked back into my normal senses and the question that should have come out of my mouth first comes rushing out in a wave,"why are you here?"

He sighs as though he would have rather kept teasing me,"long story short," he whispers and it's an active effort for me not to get distracted by his adams apple,"I got caught, but," he adds before I attack him,"good news it was Quincy and so I told her everything and now she's joined us and is taking care of Tay as we speak. So I could come help you."

"You. Are. A. IDIOT!" I hiss,"I don't need your help!"

"Liar." His head sweeps even closer." you always need my help. Besides now you can have back up after you get back from the assassination.

"You shouldn't have just left him with Quincy!"

Jax's voice hardens,"I know you trust Quincy. And I trust her too. I know you probably don't need me. But I wasn't just about to double babysit if I wasn't needed."

"Fine," I say,"After the cry goes out that the King is dead, go get Tay as soon as possible."

Jax gins, "Your wish is my command."

CHAPTER 9

The palace is huge and to no surprise the inside is furnished and painted in all white inside as well.

Not that I'm on the inside anyway.

With Conrad above me we scale the outside shingling effortlessly up to the Kings balcony. Every once in a whale I'm able to glance into a window seeing the inside.

Up here the wind is ruthless.

My shoulder aching in a way I've told myself is pleasant, the poison and weapons strapped to me aren't helping.

I reach up for a white shingle of the castle, but to my shock it comes off. The wind takes away all sound of my scream as I lose both my grip and my footing falling backwards.

In the split second before falling I force myself to stay calm positioning my body so when I fall I scrape against the siding. I dig into the building with my fingernails forcing myself not to feel the pain in several of them cracking down the middle and one even coming off.

"There's no time to catch your breath."

I look up to see Conrad hasn't even bothered looking down to see if I'm alright.

Not letting myself ponder this I force myself to begin moving up the side once more.

I've never gone on a mission during the middle hours of early morning and I feel with every movement that a crossbow arrow is going to find its way through my tight armor even though I know that all of the guards have been apprehended, I don't bother to think how.

After what feels like forever we reach the balcony to the kings chambers, blood trickles down my arm from my cracked nails.

Conrad takes his lovely time climbing over and my arms I have to take deep breaths from carrying both Conrad and my own weapons.

Conrad doesn't reach an arm down for me so using pure will power I muscle my way up.

My breath comes out in short ragged gasps.

"You're getting clumsy, once I take the throne I don't believe you will be resizing my star spot anymore."

I purse my lips knowing he doesn't want a response.

He looks at me over,"maybe I will consider you once you lose a little weight, you're getting fat, Jax might lose his interest as well."

At this moment I'd gladly let Jax put an arrow through this man's heart.

It takes everything in me not to try to kill him right there.

This time when I speak my words aren't ragged because I'm out of breath,"I don't believe this is time for this conversation."

"I've learned to enjoy killing. Maybe this will help you. Prolonging the anticipation."

All I let myself do is nod and think about how in a few hours all that this man has ever worked for will die,"you're probably right."

"Correction, I am right."

Not meeting his eyes I simply nod.

There's a moment of silence. I feel his eyes burning into me before I finally meet his gaze. He gives me a smirking smile as he leans back against the balcony looking at the door to the Kings bedchamber.

He prolongs the moment before giving me the signal.

I pull my hood over my face and silently move to the doors.

Predictably the doors are locked.

"Open the door for me once inside." Conrad says leaning against the balcony edge.

Instead of picking the lock like an amateur I haul myself up to the small ledge above the door where a small window is unlocked I push it down more slipping into the large dark room filled with the sound of breathing.

Still perched on the small ledge inside of the room I look down at the couple sleeping in the bed.

Despite hearing about him for years and visiting his house regularly I've never acutely seen the King up close before.

He's a rather fat man the same age as Conrad but not even close to as handsome, with his gray hair full of bald splotches, and wrinkled skin.

The woman next to him however looks at least ten years younger, with a ripe complexion and long golden hair twisted in the man's fingers.

The King's first wife who gave birth to Tay, died eight years ago after the King had her killed so he could blame it on Conrad. The fact that it enabled him to be with a much younger woman, who he never bothered marrying, didn't hurt either..

Slipping down from my perch I walk to the bed. I know Conrad is waiting for me to open the door for him but I know if I do he'll have me kill this innocent woman as well.

Just like I did with Tay I take out my small pill of night-lock, breaking it and feeding her just enough to put her out for a few hours.

After the nightlock is in her system I do the same to the King, screw what Conrad will say.

Using all of my strength I haul her body off of the bed trying to be as silent as possible as I stuff her in their large closet.

Finally, finally with the King drugged and asleep I open the door for Conrad.

He struts in as though this is his own bedchamber and I've been using it for a little too long.

"I got stuck on the ledge." I lie, seeing he's about to ask why I took ages.

His face contorts,"Lose weight and you won't get stuck anymore."

Don't hurt him, Isha.

Don't.

Conrad takes a deep breath,"This is what power smells like, breathe it in."

I hold my breath.

With controlled movements I follow Conrad to loom above the drugged sleeping man.

"What would you like to use?" I ask him, motioning to the weapons on my back while simultaneously ignoring the deep pit in my stomach.

For the briefest of moments something flashes in Conrad's eyes that I've never seen on his face before, it looks like...Fear.

He's afraid of actually doing dirty work himself.

He's a coward.

That's all you are Conrad, I think, a coward and a bully.

"I am going to watch." He says replacing fear with malice.

I don't bother to argue, but I also don't bother to argue with the fear and guilt I feel every time before a kill.

"Wait," Conrad commands quietly,"wake him first."

I know for a fact that with the nightlock in his veins he won't wake up.

But I can't let Conrad know this.

So before Conrad can somehow wake him and bully him into a fearful, painful death, I stab the blades deep into his breathing chest.

Conrad goes dead quite as I pull my blades out of his chest.

For some reason I'm not afraid of the misery I'm about to deal with from Conrad. There's an odd sort of fredom I feel at disobeying Conrad for the first time.

Not everybody can walk through hell and survive. But I'm not everybody so I'm going to do it with a smile.

Sometimes quiet is more dangerous than yelling. Anticipation for what Conrads going to do to me after disobeying him follows me back down the edge of the building.

I'm still waiting as Conrad tells all of the remaining troops to attack Castle just after we get the news of the

King's death, then everybody will be weak and it will be easy to take control.

After everybody's sitting back waiting Conrad tells me to come see him deeper in the woods.

Without words I follow.

CHAPTER 10

In a clearing in the woods Conrad turns his frosty eyes on me.

I am completely aware of the fact that I'm about to be severely injured.

"Do you know what it's like to work hard for something, Isha?"

I hate questions that aren't questions.

"Because I do." Conrad slowly comes closer to me as he speaks,"Imagine." He takes another step closer,"that you have." Another step, "worked your whole insignificant life for something," step,"and your moment has finally come," another step,"but you don't even get time to fully do your work." He is right in front of me now,"because somebody ruined it. How would you feel, Isha?"

I look dead straight into his eyes,"then I'd screw myself for making other people do all the dirty work for me."

I don't bother trying to protest against his punch when it comes. Conrad rarely hits us. But when he does, every once in a while, he will make sure we keep fearing him, he makes us remember it.

But if I was afraid of pain though I would have tried to dodge.

I take the pain as it comes. I let my body curl in on itself, and tears eventually sting my eyes.

After a few minutes I start to see black and wonder if I've finally pushed this man off of the edge.

I should have just let him torture to King, it's not like the King is a good man anyway. Both him and Conrad are horrible.

But they're still both human.

As another kick and punch hit me I thank the stars that Jax is helping me and can still take down Conrad.

As another kick hits me death feels near.

My eye's squeeze out another set of tears.

Conrad doesn't deserve my tears.

"Get your bloody hands off of her!"

A voice cuts through Conrad's abuse.

My head is too hurt to recognize it.

"Get out of here Jax!" I always recognize Conrad's voice though.

"Get away from her."

The other voice is pure malice.

"Leave or I'll have you killed."

"If you so much as touch her again, I'll kill you!"

Another hard kick sends jolts across my abdomen.

I'm sent unconscious before I can hear the other man's next words.

I wake to somebody holding me against their chest.

My head hurts so badly it feels like somebody has run a knife through it.

Whoever is holding me feels so good there that I don't want to bother opening my eyes.

I must stir because the voice of the man who must have sent away Conrad comes to me gently,"Isha? Are you awake."

Forcing my eyes to open I look up to see Jax staring down at me.

I breath in his strong and beautiful eyes before forcing myself to sit up. It takes almost all of my strength to do so, but he makes sure I'm steady before letting me move away from him.

"Thank you." I croak, wishing my voice didn't sound so shaken.

Jax's voice sounds deadly as he forces his words out,"you shouldn't have to thank me. You shouldn't ever have someone treat you like that." He spits out the last word.

I remember the time he merely offered to kill the prince for me and Conrad tortured him for it.

I feel intense guilt now for not even thinking about the amount of time Conrad must have tortured Jax.

"I should have just killed him now."

"We need his death to be public so the other gang leaders won't immediately take Conrad's place."

As my eyes begin to focus more I notice now the blood streaming down from above Jax's eyebrow and his beat up lip.

"You're bleeding." I reach my hand out trying to dab away the blood.

"You're no pretty sight yourself, sweetheart."

I ignore this, closing my eyes to hide the tears,"you shouldn't have gotten involved."

Jax lets out an ignorant laugh but it's not his usual laugh. This laugh is cruel and hard,"he was going to kill you, Isha."

"No he wasn't." I say my head throbbing,"but now we might not be able to get inside the castle because Conrads mad at us."

"Screw that. I wasn't going to just stand there and let him hurt you."

I roll my eyes which hurts more than it should,"he's hurt all of us Jax. If you think that was the first time then get out of your own head."

Real anguish crosses his face and when he speaks his words sound broken,"I'm so so sorry you've had to grow up with that man leading us."

I'm surprised by this so I try to soften my voice for my next words,"It's fine Jax he's-"

"No! It's not fine Isha!" His eyes flash,"It's never fine to go onto the streets, take kids who need help, bring them in then scare them into doing what you want! That's not fine in any world!"

I look down, not meeting his eyes.

In this split second moment I realize something. Something I should have seen years ago. Jax is an amazing human being. Yes, maybe he flirts too much and maybe he can be a jerk at times and annoying, but when it comes down to it. He's a good person, no, an amazing person.

"I just wish it didn't take you kidnapping a little boy and killing so many people for me to finally start fighting him." I whisper.

Making myself meet his hurt eyes I say in a hushed tone,"At least we're starting now. Now," I make my voice lose its emotion and move farther away from him wishing his eyes weren't so intent on me,"is everybody still out there?"

He shakes his head,"No, after Conrad ran away he's taken them to siege the palace in its moment of weakness."

"So... Quincy has Tay..." My mind starts working to remember the plan we've formed over the past week,"Do you think Conrad will welcome us back?"

Jax nods,"you go get Quicny to bring Tay to this forest by then the main fighting should be over and Conrad will come out to give his speech, then will kill him and bring Tay forward to become the next King."

"What will you do?" I ask.

He gives me his usual grin but it's sad,"I'll go join the fight so Conrad will see I'm still loyal."

Right before he leaves I suddenly lunge towards him giving him a hug. I notice he barely hugs me back so before he can say a word I move away awkwardly.

Before running into the woods.

CHAPTER 11

J ax P.O.V.

It's not bad enough that I had to fake kiss her today.

No, then I had to see Conrad hurting her.

When I saw him hurting her I could barely keep my cool.

Correction.

I didn't keep my cool.

It's been bad enough all these years just knowing he hurts her, not only physically, but seeing her every time she can home after a mission. How broken her eyes looked.

I just couldn't do it. Seeing him there.

Touching her.

Anger rises in my chest just thinking about it.

And as if all of this isn't bad enough for one day, she's now hugging me.

I can't count the amount of times I've daydreamed about me gently touching her.

But not like this.

Not when I know if I hug her back, I won't be able to let her go, that I'll need to take the time to run my fingers through her black hair, and trace my finger over her spine.

I already almost lost it with that kiss.

And I know she doesn't want that.

So I don't say a word to her as she leaves me.

Sighing I turn in the opposite direction towards the palace.

I'm the only person who seems to be walking towards the palace as people from every direction seem to be trying to get as far away from it as they can.

Even the guards from the palace seem to be running.

The closer I get to the Palace the more bodies litter the streets, Conrad doesn't take prisoners.

Sighing I move into to join the fight for the wrong side.

No kidding, it takes four hours of hard fighting before Conrad has taken the palace as his own and had everybody who was loyal to the old throne line murdered or locked up for questioning.

An hour after that scouts are sent out to declare to all the land they have a new king.

As the other gang leaders begin commanding everyone to clean up and do other tasks I keep a careful eye on Conrad. To my surprise Conrad doesn't acknowledge me. But I guess he can't send me away or else people will find out that I beat him at something.

Conrad says he won't give his speech to the people until the scouts have told all of the people to come watch tomorrow morning.

Immediately I think of Isha bringing Tay back to the palace and realize I need to get to the woods as soon as possible.

Unfortunately before I can I'm intercepted by Leela and Janner who come up to me smiling as though nothing out of the ordinary has happened today.

They're both good people deep down but they're just dumb.

The only reason I've put up with them for so long is because I don't know how to live without other people's friendship.

"We're finally living the big life!" Leela grins laughing.

"Um sure." I say kind of distracted at the moment wishing I had known that the speech would be tomorrow so we hadn't gotten Quincy to be coming to the woods right now.

"What's wrong man?" Janner cuts in, his eyes suspicious.

I turn to him, taking a chance, "do you guys ever get tired of the killing? Don't you guys wish that we hadn't spent all of our lives with Conrad just killing? Like don't you think there's a better way to handle things?"

All I'm given in response is blank judging faces.

Leela smiles with sympathy, "you seem like you need a drink, J. Let's go find an open bar."

I can't believe these are the only people I got to be with before Isha joined me. But I tell them I'm off to go find a bar so I'll have a good reason to leave the palace. It doesn't even occur to them that zero bars are going to be open at 3 in the afternoon right after a huge attack on the city's capital was just waged.

Why have I put up with them for so long?

Chapter 12

It's hot even as the sun sets. I'm not sure whether I should bring Quincy and Stay with me up to the palace or not...

After a minute or two I decided to keep them in the woods instead of bringing them up.

Just to be safe.

I walk up to the palace gates as I do scared people on the street look at me with pure terror.

At the gates the two gang members recognize me and I feel so odd about just walking into this palace that it takes me a second to realize that Conrads in control now.

I feel guilty about how deep down it feels good to not have to live in fear of being caught.

I push that feeling down.

As I walk through the halls not really knowing where I'm going I catch a glimpse of myself in a mirror.

Dang.

I look like a bleeding mess.

Bruises are forming on my face, neck and collarbones and dried blood coats my chin and eyebrows.

I also try to hide the limp as I walk.

I walk until I find somebody I recognize.

It's Leela.

I hate how pretty she is in a plump blonde girl sort of way.

"Hello." I say in greeting.

"Oh hey." She says, sounding less than happy to see me.

"Do you know where Jax is?"

I get glare for mentioning her crush.

"Yeah," her voice is smug,"he went to get a drink."

Screw that boy.

"Oh." I say lamely.

Why would he go get a drink when we're about to go watch the speech!

"But isn't everybody supposed to go watch Conrad's speech?"

She looks at me like I'm a disgusting puppy she found on the side of the road."It's tomorrow. Conrad literally just told us all that."

Her eye's skirt over my beat up appearance and her nose wrinkles,"I guess you might be avoiding Conrad though."

I bleeding hate her.

She sighs,"you should go to the west wing, that's where all of us are supposed to stay."

I nod curtly.

"Thank you." Is all I can manage.

I race back to the woods to tell Quincy she needs to take Tay and hide until tomorrow morning when the speech is. But when I reach the woods she's already gone. I search around the wood for a while until I find a note carved into a tree. So subtly you wouldn't notice unless you were looking everywhere like I am.

We're fine. See you tomorrow.

Q.

Quincy must somehow have heard that she has to come back tomorrow.

How? I have no idea.

But at least she's safe.

CHAPTER 13

The house I've spent more than half my life in is beautiful, but it doesn't even come close to the beauty of this palace.

The room I'm directed to is massive.

In comparison to the King's chambers, where I have no doubt Conrad is staying, it's a tiny room but everything you have always looks small in comparison to something else.

I marvel at the small private bathroom which I fill to the brim with hot fuchsia colored water.

My hair and body are given the best rinse of their life.

It's pure luxury to let the dirt and grime come off me.

To let my tight muscles loosen against the burning water.

I spend at least an hour in the tub till the water runs cold before I put on a bathrobe, letting my hair fall wet on my shoulders.

To my surprise the closet has clothing in it.

Only after I put on a green dress with straps that cross over my shoulders and lower back, do I realize that this room just a day before most likely belonged to a handmaiden now evicted from her home in order for me to be here...

The thought leaves me feeling odd on the inside.

After I'm changed my stomach growls reminding me to eat.

I join a group of girls from one of Conrad's smaller outcroppings who I don't know for dinner.

We all eat plain chicken and salad.

Apparently we can all have nice rooms and clothing but we're still only Conrad's monkeys, and pets have to be kept on a chain.

After tomorrow what will happen to all of these people?

What will happen to the councilmen down in dungeons?

Who will me and Jax become after tomorrow?

I don't eat much at dinner, perturbed by my thoughts and am the first one to leave.

I can't wait to get back to my room in perfect solitude and sleep in that big fluffy bed.

Just as I round the corner of our hallway I'm stopped.

Jax is leaning against my door frame with his first few buttons undone lazily staring at me.

"What do you want?" My voice comes out too harsh.

Jax looks surprised,"I wanted too..." He trails off,"did I do something?"

"No." I snap, but it's a lie.

He tries to give me his warmest smile but all he gets is another glare.

"C'on Isha, tell me what I did so I can apologize."

I give him a sweet smile too,"I hope you had a fun time going out and getting drinks when you should have been here. But I'm glad you've had a fun few hours out on the town just doing whatever you like!"

I try to push past him but he throws out one arm.

"What the crap Isha," He actually looks angry now even though he has no right to get mad at me. "Do you really think I would just leave?" He lowers his voice, "I went to tell Quincy to go hide until tomorrow morning! I wasn't drinking! I wasn't out kissing random girls! I was helping! Because as shocking as it is, to you. I'm not just some jerk who has no moral compass!"

Embarrassment floods my cheeks at the real hurt in his eyes,"You just- I mean- Leela said you- I just was mad because we have important things to do and you just-"

He holds up a hand to stop me,"screw whatever the heck petty little Leela said! I just can't believe you think I'd leave you," his voice breaks,"after all I've done this week- I thought you trusted me."

"I'm sorry- but maybe you shouldn't have the type of reputation where I could believe something like that!"

He shakes his head, his blonde hair flopping into his eyes,"whatever, I'll see you tomorrow. Oh and," he turns, still looking hurt,"tomorrow after we kill Conrad, Quincy will bring Tay to the palace. I just thought you'd want to know what's happening."

He's gone before I can get a hold of my raging emotions.

CHAPTER 14

There's a girl in my room.

I've never seen her in my life, meaning she's from another group.

"Oh! Hi!" Says the blonde girl.

"Why are you in my room?" I'm too tired to sound nice.

"I'm your roommate!"

"My what?"

"You know a person who you share a room w-"

"I know what a roommate is! I'm just wondering why the heck I have a roommate!"

She smiles,"Conrad can't have us take up too much space."

Oh. Of course his little pets can't have their own rooms.

The girl smiles again, I hate blonde people's smiles,"I decided I want the bed, because I got here first and all."

I look around the room,"I'm not sleeping on the ground."

"Then where will you sleep?" She sounds legitimately concerned.

She giggles,"But I have the bed silly."

I'm too tired to fight.

Ignoring the stupid blonde, I head towards the closet to find something to sleep in.

"I just divided the clothes, you can have all of the stuff on the left."

Opening the closet door I see a row of beautiful well fitted dresses, shirts, and underclothing.

On the left there is a pile of dirty brown day dresses.

"Oh! By the way, just put the dress you are wearing on my side!"

Instead of picking up one of 'my' dresses I pick out the best looking night dress and get changed into it putting the dress I was wearing into my pile as well as several other dresses.

When I get out Stupid Blonde says,"Who was that boy standing by our door?"

I will punch this girl in the face if she keeps talking to me,"He's married with two kids." I lie.

That shuts her up. Until she looks over at me,"Hey, that was in my pile."

"Was it?" I say yawning.

"Yes!"

Before I can do anything she charges me.

Freaking charges at me,"Give it back!" She screams.

Still with a yawn I flip her me smacking her hard into the ground.

When I look down, her body lays unconscious.

She's a lot better this way.

Finally I go to bed.

Even though a few minutes later before the lights turn out I feel a sharp little hand smack me on the head before she falls asleep on the floor crying about a jerk I am.

Chapter 15

I wake before Stupid blonde in the morning and get showered and dressed before her eyes even begin to sneak open.

I make my way to the Library of the Palace.

The speech isn't until noon so I have time to kill.

Quicny is going to sneak Tay in while me and Jax kill Conrad before putting the baby king forward.

I pick up a history book, obviously biased for the King's favor and begin flipping through it.

Only after I've read a good three chapters do I realize not a word of what I've read has sunk in.

With a sigh I re-shelve the book.

My mind flips over to Jax, he's probably still mad at me.

I really was a bloody jerk last night.

I smack my head with my palm cursing my fat mouth.

It's an hour before Conrad's speech is to take place, and citizens are already beginning to be herded into the court-yard.

The speech is taking place on the seventh floor balcony so Conrad can address all of his new subjects with his power.

I make my way to the seventh floor where the large balcony protrudes from the building.

Conrad's already standing outside the two large doors leading out onto the balcony, along with his many guards and assassins. He's dressed in dark purple clothing with a crown draped across his forehead. As I watch him I realize he can never truly look like a king. No matter what Conrad wears or says it can't hid the fact that the something deep within Conrad is missing from him. The part that makes you deeply respect a king. I'll never respect Conrad. All I see when I look at him is a coward.

As though he knows I'm thinking of him, Conrad's eyes meet mine for a split second as I enter the room.

His mouth peaks into a cunning smile as his eyes trace the bruises on my collarbone and face.

With my head held strong I stand where I'm directed.

Jax told me not to worry about how he's going to take care of Conrad, all I know is it's going to be in a very public way.

When Jax enters it feels like all heads swivel to him.

To be fair I understand why.

Even with his busted lip he looks beautiful.

Next to him and behind him walk in Leela along with my dumb blonde roommate.

He leans over and says something that makes Dumb Blonde laugh.

I kind of want to scratch her eyes out.

CHAPTER 16

Ten minutes till the speech and all of us are in position right outside of the balcony doors. There's a hum in the air that feels electric.

I take a deep breath. Everything is about to be alright.

Conrad will die and the real king will be put on the throne.

Everything will be just fine.

Except it won't... Because if we kill Conrad we'll be just like Conrad.

Killing to get what we want.

It will be no better than if Conrad himself took the throne... If Conrad dies this will be the beginning of a new age, but I don't want a new age that was born in blood.

And killing.

And killing.

Killing.

Killing.

My word blood seems to run cold in my blood as I make a decision.

I turn to try and find Jax so I can speak with him but before I can Conrad motions all of us forward out to the balcony.

Cold coils in my chest as one final plan blooms in my mind

If I'm the only life that is lost by doing this, then so be it.

What's one more scar from a blade?

On the balcony blank faces stare at us from below where thousands of cowering people just want to go home.

My breaths are short and uneven.

I'm afraid.

Why am I always so bloody afraid?

I try to catch Jax's eye but he won't look my way.

Conrad grins down at everyone below. "People of Mondon!" He shouts, "I am here to give you the freedom you deserve from your old leader! When you look at me now, see the god I am! See freedom, see pride!"

The only thing I see is the knife Jax just unsheathe from his belt.

Jax takes a step.

I think I'm the only one to notice Jax moving slowly towards Conrad.

He takes another step.

I can't let him kill Conrad!

Another.

Yes you can! Conrad is a multiplicative monster.

Some eyes turn to Jax but nobody does anything.

So? Not all monsters deserve to die!

Jax lifts the knife higher.

Yes they do!

Nobody says a thing.

Then why aren't you dead?

Jax starts to swing down the blade-

"Stop!" My scream comes out like somebody just physically hurt me, the echo of that single word parades around the room as all eyes turn to me.

Conrad whips around fury burning a black hole in his eyes.

Jax looks at me with confusion as blood drains from his face.

I run forward without thinking, shoving Conrad aside. To my shock he moves.

I turn to the crowd knowing I have thirty seconds tops before Conrad takes me down.

"Prince Tay is alive!" I ignore the gasps from everybody and go on,"I was the one meant to kill him but I saved his life instead!"

"What are you doing?" Jax hisses next to me.

"I saved him because I saw the future that would happen if Conrad rules, he will kill everybody who stands in his way to getting more power! We will live a life with more fear and pain! And what kind of future is that?"

Murmurs break out.

"Get down!" Conrad roars, the most of an outbreak I've ever seen him have in public.

I ignore him looking desperately over the crowd,"help me restore the prince to the throne! Please, we need peace not hate and fear we need-"

I hear it before I feel it.

The ice cold sound of a blade.

"ISHA!" Jax yells.

Before I can turn around somebody in the crowd screams.

Everybody screams.

A piercing white pain hits my world so deeply that I can barely breath.

I turn around to see Conrad evenly pulling his hand away.

Hands rush to me, it's Jax.

I look down.

I look back at Jax.

I hear a stampede of people.

Jax is crying.

People are shouting.

I am crying.

Pain.

Pain when Jax pulls out the dagger from my stomach.

It's his dagger.

Pain.

My eyes see black.

I collapse but not before I see fear in Conrad's eyes and a crowd of people from below rushing the palace.

So much for peace.

I'm in and out of consciousness.

There's red everywhere.

And so much noise.

And pain.

Until suddenly it's gone.

The noise. Not the pain.

I hear desperate voices yelling.

Then two comforting ones.

"You're going to be fine honey."

It's Quincy .

I love Quincy .

"I'm going to go kill him, Quincy. Mark my words, if that man lives I burn the world just to see him die."

It's Jax.

I think I might love Jax too.

But I can't let people die.

"Don't kill," is all I can manage. I did all of this just so we wouldn't have to kill anymore.

"She said something!" Jax's arms are around me,"what?" His voice is gentle.

"I said don't kill them-" It's all I can manage before I slip into another darkness.

"I said don't kill them-" It's all I can manage before I slip into another darkness.

Chapter 17

J ax P.O.V.

He's going to die for hurting her again.
I don't care what Isha thinks I should do.
Conrad is going to die today.
And I'm going to enjoy killing him.

Chapter 18

The war P.O.V.

The people charged the castle to save their prince. The prince cried because he watched one of his only friends be in pain.

An evil man lived because a good girl decided not to be weak.

A strong blonde haired boy fought with the people for their justice.

A strong blonde haired boy saw an evil man, the evil man looked at the boy.

It seemed to be just them in the midst of a storm.

An evil man ran.

A strong boy chased.

An evil man was caught and realized he was going to die.

A strong boy knew he was going to kill an evil man.

A strong boy thought of a strong dying girl.

He thought of her words.

A stronger boy became stronger.

An evil man who lived his life hurting others was not hurt, but he received a present he never gave.

Mercy.

That day a fight was fought.

That day an evil man and his few evil people who learned the beauty of a kill were thrown into a prison of living hell.

That day a prince was crowned a king.

That day people went home, some to a newly broken family other to whole ones.

That day a new legacy was born.

That day a kingdom born in blood and hate was newly made in forgiveness.

That day was today.

CHAPTER 19

A week after the Siege

Click.

Clack.

Click.

Clack.

I'm lying on something soft.

My body is cocooned in a soft blanket.

I feel newly regenerated.

My eyes open to see a room streaming with morning light.

"Ish!"

"What dear?"

"Ish! Ish! Ish is awake!"

To my great surprise I see Tay leaping up and down.

"Ish! Guess what! Y-you were like asleep for a really long time and Jax he cried a lot and he he said that he loved you and he was so sad and I was sad to but I was still brave and their was a big fight but now we're all happy and that bad man is in jail and we all happy!"

I stare at his little dark face and frizzy hair, what in the crap happened.

"Get away from the poor girl."

My eyes brim with tears as I look up to see Quincy smiling down at me with love.

Then we're both crying and she's hugging me into her large bosom.

"I thought you were dying!" She cries.

"I thought I was dying too!" I half cry half laugh back.

We stay like this until Tay decides to join us too, wiggling his little body in between us.

"Tell me what happend?" I ask Quincy.

"Yes, but first eat."

So as I eat she tells me how the people charged the palace after Conrad stabbed me. How they fought to get Tay on the throne, she tells me how Conrad is now living in prison along with his few most trusted guards. How they held a coronation for Tay and decided that if I lived I would be his counselor until he turns sixteen.

My jaw drops,"but-but I'm not qualified to rule a country! I can't be his advisor!"

"Do you not want to be?"

I think about her question,"who would take my place?"

She smiles, still wiping away tears,"that's why we gave it to you."

"I guess I'll have to then."

"You won't be alone, dear."

"Speaking of alone..." My voice trails off wanting to ask the question in my mind since I woke up.

"Yes?" Her eyes glint.

"Where's... Jax?"

Suddenly Quincy throws her knitting in the air. "I'm done." She simply says.

"What?" I look at her confused.

"I'm done." She says again promptly,"I'm done keeping this secret from both of you."

"What secret?"

"You heard Tay say it earlier, Jax has been so bleeding in love with you for years that he just about died this week and I know you have feelings for him so don't say a word."

The only thing I think to say is,"Jax is not in love with me! Why would he be in love with me?"

"Don't give yourself a stroke, and I don't bleeding know why he's in love with you but he's been head over heels for a year or two now."

"But.... he never said anything!"

Quincy rolls her eyes,"yes and he's been complaining to me about it."

I look around the room as though he might just suddenly appear,"where is he?"

Quincy's face looks sympathetic, "He left a half hour ago saying how he just couldn't do it anymore. I don't know what that means."

Jax loved me all this time and I've been being mean to him for years.... And now he's gone.

I sit up and pain shoots threw my back reminding me of the healing wound.

"Am I alright to go find him?"

"I'm not a doctor but I know I won't be able to stop you if I were."

Before she's even finished her sentence I'm out the door. Ignoring the pain, shooting threw me with each step.

It takes longer than I'd like but finally somebody tells me they saw Jax leave fifteen minutes ago.

I try to find my way to the exit of this bleeding castle while being in intense pain but I keep getting stopped.

Apparently now I'm famous for being a girl who was brave enough to get a thousand people to attack a palace of armed assassins, then get stabbed in the stomach and pass out.

I'm just so heroic.

By the time I get out of the castle I am positive Jax is far away.

I race along the road in the direction I was told Jax was going, praying I'll find him.

And suddenly there he is. And he has a bag in one hand.

He's leaving.

For good.

He's leaving and he's never going to come back.

He was just going to leave me.

"Wait!"

Jax's tall form whips around, shock emulating on his face,"Isha?"

In my rush to see him. I'd planned a whole list of things to say to him but now that he's here in front of me I just start to cry, full on bawling and shaking because I'm just so relieved that he's here in front of me.

"Please don't go." I try to wipe the tears away from my eye,"I'm so sorry I'm always so mean to you, and I'm a jerk when you always just try to be nice to me. I'm so sorry that I do annoying things, but I really do love you. So please don't go because I don't think I could actually live with myself if you left." Why won't these tears bleeding stop? "And I'm just such a stupid idiot for not telling you this sooner or realizing that," I take a big old gasp of air,"that you really are one of my very best friends, and somehow you became my best friend without me even realizing it. But I also think I might love you, so just please don't go."

Jax stares at me for a long moment. Then without a word he runs to me, dropping his bag, his arms encircling me. His arms are gentle around me but even with him so close I can't stop sniffling and sobbing tears getting mixed with snot on him.

"Please don't leave me." I sniffle.

His hand strokes my hair as he lets out a short laugh."I wasn't leaving you. I just went to get something to eat outside of the castle, you over dramatic princess."

I'm still crying. "You mean you were going to come back?"

"Yeah."

"Promise?"

"Promise."

There is a moment where he's just holding me and still crying as I say as my tears subside,"Quincy said that you..." I'm not really sure how to finish that sentence and I'm almost positive I said I was in love with him earlier.

"What did she say?" His voice comes out a little bit panicked.

"She.. uh she said that you um have liked me for a really long time..."

It's awkward as he lets go of me to run a hand through his hair.

"Stupid Quincy," he mutters partly to himself,"don't ever tell her you secrets."

"But you never seemed like you liked me! I mean we're always fighting," I point out.

Except for when we're not fighting and we actually have fun, or acutely talk to each other.

He frowns at me,"you haven't exactly always been lining up to have long chats with me have you? The only way I could get to talk to you was fighting."

I open my mouth then close it,"but why?"

"Why what?"

"Why do you like me?" It feels weird saying it in present tense,"And since when?"

He laughs as though he finds the thought of not liking me impossible,"I've liked you since I met you."

"But I was fourteen!"

"You were a hot fourteen year old."

I give him a glare making him laugh again.

"Na, I'm just kidding. You annoyed the crap out of me when I first met you."

"Wow thanks."

"But over the last year or two... I don't know.... I just sort of started always wanting you around. Sometimes I'd ask Conrad to put us on missions together, or stuff like that. But I guess I've just always sort of thought you were interesting."

"Interesting." I say, not impressed.

He shrugs,"yeah, I like the way you say things I think is interesting, I don't really get how your brain works, and I like the challenge of figuring it out. Also you're smarter than me, which is annoying sometimes. Also." He adds, grinning down at me,"is it too shallow of me to say I just think you're gorgeous. And don't you dare ask me to explain why I think you're gorgeous because then you'd hate me."

I laugh and then I'm crying again.

Jax looks scared,"I'm sorry, I didn't mean to-"

"No." I interrupt,"I'm happy."

Then I'm hugging him again.

I glance at his chest,"I'm ruining your shirt." I say through my tears.

"I don't like this anyway."

"You're lying." I sniffle,"you wear that shirt all the time."

He laughs now too.

"Jax?"

"Yes." He says softly.

"They want me to lead until Tay is sixteen."

"I know."

"Jax?"

"Yes?"

"Will you help me lead?"

"Of course but we already covered the fact that you're smarter than me."

I give him a huge smile in between the silence.

"Isha?"

"Yeah?"

"Can I kiss you right now, or will I get an attempted death threat?"

"If I were to threaten your life it would be real."

"Was that a yes?"

"Did it sound like a yes?"

"...No."

"Yes."

"Was that a yes?"

"What do you think?"

I kiss him.

And this time it's completely real.

EPILOGUE

S ix years later.

Jax almost always wakes up before me.

Which is fine with him because he likes to cuddle and fine with me because I like to get my sleep.

But today I wake up first.

I glance down at my Jax, his blonde hair a mess across our pillows, his wedding band gleaming on his

I take a deep breath, trying not to think about today.

I know I'm more nervous than Tay, who doesn't even seem to care that the entire weight of a kingdom is being completely put on his shoulders today as I step away from being his legal guardian and overseer of the country.

Over the past years, if I hadn't had Jax by my side, the weight of a kingdom on my shoulders might have killed me.

Ceremoniously, I wack Jax on the head, "Wake up!" I say cheerily.

He moans, rolling over and raping his arm around my waist, tracing the new little bump in my stomach, "I feel like not doing that."

"Too bad; today is important."

"You say that every day."

"Today, I mean it."

"You mean you don't always mean it! You've been lying to me all this time?" He gasps snuggling closer.

"Yep, too bad." I run my fingers through his hair, which makes him sigh.

He sits up then, "You aren't thinking about becoming a dictator and not giving Tay the crown, are you?"

"No! Of course not."

"Good, because I want to retire and not have to share you with this bloody country anymore."

"Twenty-six-year-olds don't get to retire."

He frowns, "Don't remind me of my old age."

I smile.

His face turns serious, "All jokes aside, stop worrying about Tay. Besides, sixteen is pretty dang mature."

"How would you know?" I raise an eyebrow.

Instead of answering, he presses his mouth against mine, pushing me back down onto the covers. A sound rises in my throat, which he swallows with his own growl as his fingers slip down my spine and_

The door flies open.

Immediately, I push Jax off of me, looking up to find Tay in the doorway, rolling his eyes.

Jax sighs dramatically. "How many bleeding times do I need to tell you to knock?"

Tay grins with a wicked smile he inherited from Jax, "How many times do I need to tell you you're too old to be so bleeding in love?"

"Shut up, both of you." I yawn, "I already have enough of a headache without the two of you yapping 24/7."

"Oh, come off it," Jax grins, winking at Tay.

"I should never have let the two of you have so much alone time together." I roll my eyes.

"I take deep offense at that." Jax gasps.

"Hopefully, pancakes will make you all feel better."

"Yes, ma'am, they will." Both Jax and Tay say as Quincy comes in with a plate full of raspberry pancakes.

Both of the boys I love most in the world sit up looking like little puppies, trying to hold still for a treat.

Quincy laughs, walking past them to me like I knew she would, "The pregnant one gets first serve."

"Unfair." They both say in unison once more.

I glare at both of them, and Jax amends his expression: "I mean of course you should get the first serving so you can feed our baby; it's my sacrifice for you."

Me and Quincy both throw pillows at Jax, which makes him laugh.

We all sit there in the morning sun eating raspberry pancakes, and later that day, as they place a crown on Tays brow, I lean into Jax watching as a boy becomes a king that hopefully we've raised to be a peacemaker.

We both watch as a kingdom bows down to their knees for their young king.

Something deep inside of me, which I didn't know was still broken, stitches itself together.

There may still be scars on my body, but today I feel the last scar on my heart disappear.

Because, unlike a broken vase glued back together, the scars of this kingdom seem to be healed.

And standing here everything feels just a little bit more perfect.